Sometimes when the road to romance turns
a little rocky, a tiny baby or toddler can help bring
two hearts together....
Read and enjoy as two couples become families in these
short-but-sweet stories from two authors who know just
how to weave a magical, touching tale....

Rebecca Winters
Adopted Baby, Convenient Wife

and

Lucy Gordon
Playboy's Surprise Son

in

And Baby Makes Three

Praise for Rebecca Winters:

"Sympathetic characters and a twist on a traditional plot
elevate this tale into something special."
—*RT Book Reviews* on *Accidentally Pregnant!*

"Rebecca Winters' *Crazy about her Spanish Boss* features a
spectacular setting and very appealing lovers."
—*RT Book Reviews*

Praise for ~~L~~

"A solid plot, multifac~~ted~~ ~~characters and a~~
central situati~~on~~

—*RT Book Review*~~s~~

"Well plotted, with an ~~...~~ practically a
character, this story has a ~~...~~ charm. It's simply delightful."
—*RT Book Reviews* on *And the Bride Wore Red*

Dear Reader,

Who can resist a baby? I know I can't. The event is miraculous. Besides bringing joy to a parent's life, the mere knowledge that a baby is on the way changes the mother's and father's worlds, not to mention those of the other family members.

A baby is born into every circumstance you can think of, and maybe some you can't! Take for example an old Western film I watched about a group of willing women being taken across the plains to meet men who wanted to get married. On the way, one of them gave birth in the covered wagon and died. When they reached their destination, another woman had fallen in love with it and claimed it for her own. The stranger husband had to take the baby, too! That's an *instant* family.

The story lived with me until one day I had to write Adopted Baby, Convenient Wife. In this novel an *instant* family is created because of one adorable, innocent baby two strangers fall in love with and can't give up. The circumstances are entirely different from the Western story, but one thing is clear: the love of a child supersedes all other considerations and can create a new miracle.

I'm delighted to be paired with the incomparable Lucy Gordon in this book *And Baby Makes Three*. I've been a fan of hers for years and deem it an honor to have a book coming out with hers. It's my hope both our stories about these precious babies will give you a few hours of pure reading pleasure.

Enjoy!

Rebecca Winters

REBECCA WINTERS

Adopted Baby, Convenient Wife

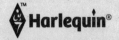

TORONTO NEW YORK LONDON
AMSTERDAM PARIS SYDNEY HAMBURG
STOCKHOLM ATHENS TOKYO MILAN MADRID
PRAGUE WARSAW BUDAPEST AUCKLAND

ISBN-13: 978-0-373-17734-9

AND BABY MAKES THREE

First North American Publication 2011

Copyright © 2011 by Harlequin Books S.A.

The publisher acknowledges the copyright
holders of the individual works as follows:

ADOPTED BABY, CONVENIENT WIFE
Copyright © 2008 by Rebecca Winters

PLAYBOY'S SURPRISE SON
Copyright © 2011 by Lucy Gordon

Recycling programs
for this product may
not exist in your area.

Rebecca Winters, whose family of four children has now swelled to include three beautiful grandchildren, lives in Salt Lake City, Utah, in the land of the Rocky Mountains. With canyons and high alpine meadows full of wild flowers, she never runs out of places to explore. They, plus her favorite vacation spots in Europe, often end up as backgrounds for her Harlequin Romance ® novels. Writing is Rebecca's passion, along with Rebecca's family and church.

She loves to hear from her readers. If you wish to email her, please visit her website at www.cleanromances.com.

CHAPTER ONE

THE wizened old cowboy filling his pickup truck at the service station in Elko tipped his hat back. "The Bonnibelle, you say?" His head turned toward the mountains. "Everyone knows it's right over there in the valley, beneath those snowcapped peaks."

Catherine had heard of it, of course, but coming from the other side of Nevada she could be forgiven for not knowing exactly where to find it.

"Biggest cattle ranch around," he expounded. "Thirty-five thousand acres. Can't miss it. After you leave town, take the 227 and follow it all the way."

Straight as the crow flies? she wanted to respond, but quashed the impulse because the older man thought he was being helpful. To his mind, he'd given her all the directions she needed.

O ye of little faith, she chided herself before thanking him. Then she got back in the car.

Having made her visit to the ladies' room, plus purchasing a cold bottle of water along with the gas, she was ready to go. But who knew how many more miles she had to travel before she reached her destination?

There wasn't any point in consulting the map she'd bought before leaving Reno. It was of no further use to her now except to tell her she was headed toward the Ruby Mountains.

In the heat waves rising from the highway, Bonnie's precious little image swam before her eyes.

If your daddy's there, my darling baby girl, I'll find him. If he's not, then I'm going to make you mine no matter what I have to do.

After losing track of time beneath a sweltering July afternoon sun blazing down on miles of rangeland, she finally spied an arch of deer antlers to her right, signifying the entrance to the Bonnibelle. A name like that must have come from the heart of some homesick Scotsman who'd settled here many years earlier and staked his claim.

It took another fifteen minutes before the dirt road climbed higher past alpine paintbrush and lupine to a crystal blue lake where an immense three-storied log ranch house hugged the shoreline. The spectacular backdrop of mountains against such splendor caused Catherine to suck in her breath.

Your daddy picked a piece of heaven when he decided to work here, sweetheart.

Beyond the main house there were clusters of immaculate outbuildings and a huge barn erected amid clumps of dark pines. Some of the structures looked as if they dated back to the second half of the 1800s.

Catherine surmised that it not only took a small army of hands to keep this place in mint condition, but a cattle king with exceptional gifts and an iron hand to make certain its inner workings ran with all the precision of a fine Swiss watch.

An odd assortment of luxury cars mixed with pickup trucks and horse trailers stood parked along the border of grass planted in front of the main house. Considering the ranch was such a big business concern, she didn't question their presence or the number of vehicles with the state's official seal decorating the car doors.

Perhaps she might have done if she hadn't been so intent on her desperate mission. With time running out, she needed to act fast. Otherwise she could lose Bonnie.

At the mere thought, stabbing pain brought fresh tears to her eyes.

The idea of someone else raising Bonnie was unthinkable to Catherine. Once she'd confirmed Bonnie's father turned out to be the no-account drifter she'd labeled him—once she heard him say he wanted nothing to do with his own flesh and blood—she was ready to go to court and claim the baby for her very own.

After finding a parking spot behind a blue Mercedes sedan, she levered herself out from the front seat of her vehicle and stepped out into the dry heat. At six thousand feet it was certainly cooler than in Elko.

Since she'd left her condo seven hours ago, the sun's position had altered. Catherine's willowy body, dressed in a crush-proof two-piece suit, cast a shadow against the bank of cars. She headed for the main entrance of the ranch house, grateful she'd worn medium-sized heels to navigate. They made a soft crunching sound on the gravel driveway.

A deep porch ran the full length of the beautiful old structure. Upon climbing the steps, she saw the sign that told visitors to ring the bell.

Not long after she'd pressed the button a maid answered the door. Catherine caught the cool breeze of the air-conditioning and welcomed it. As she breathed in, she detected the strong scent of fresh flowers.

Beyond the young woman she noticed several massive sprays of roses and lilies placed at either side of the bottom of the grand staircase. The interior of the spacious foyer had more the look of an English manor than its rustic western exterior conveyed.

While Catherine was wondering if she'd interrupted a wedding or some such thing, the maid said, "Everyone's gathered in the great room. If you'd like to follow me."

"Oh, but I'm not—"

Catherine stopped talking because the maid had already disappeared through two paneled doors on the right, leaving

Catherine in a dilemma. Whatever social event she'd walked in on, she hadn't been invited.

Making a decision to err on the side of caution, she hurried outside again. She would wait in her car until she saw someone leave the ranch house. At that point she would approach them to find out what was going on. Depending on the answer, she might have to double back to Elko for the night and return in the morning.

Her reasons for coming here were private and personal. After suffering a troubled childhood and teenage years, Catherine had been given a second chance at life. Now, years later, she was in a position to fight for someone who couldn't.

The problem was, any information she gave to the wrong person could jeopardize everything. She refused to let that happen, not when she'd made promises to Terrie she intended to keep.

"Mr. Farraday?"

"Excuse me, Hal," Cole said to the Lieutenant Governor and his aide before turning to face Janine, the newest member of the household staff. The tone in her voice held a certain nuance that prompted him to walk her over to one of the windows where they could be apart from the thirty or so people left in the room. "What is it, Janine?"

"A woman I've never seen before came to the door just now. I assumed she must be a friend of the family, so I asked her to come in and follow me."

Making that kind of assumption was Janine's first mistake, but Cole let her continue uninterrupted.

"When I turned around, she was gone! I don't know if she's somewhere in the house, or if she left. I alerted Mack, but thought you should know."

Cole schooled his dark features not to reveal his thoughts. "You did the right thing to come to me. Give me a description."

"She was a tallish blonde wearing a yellow outfit."

"How old?"

Janine shrugged her shoulders. "Maybe twenty-five, twenty-six."

Or maybe thirty-five, thirty-six, all disguised by a series of surgical makeovers? One of Buck's bimbos from the past? Some exotic dancer his thirty-year-old brother had gotten involved with at an XXX-rated bar in Elko before he'd cleaned up his act?

Buck had the kind of looks women couldn't resist. He came from money and was always ready for a good time. For the last few years it had taken everything Cole and his brother John could do to keep Buck's nocturnal activities under wraps. In secret, Cole had even asked his uncle Richard, who lived in Reno, to take Buck under his wing for the latter part of last summer in the hope of straightening him out.

He smothered a groan of protest, because this woman had dared to trespass even though she knew Buck had married Lucy two months ago. That was all his shattered sister-in-law needed right now.

He knew how she felt. Ten years ago Cole had lost his wife, Jenny, and his dream of a family of his own had died with her. Maybe the Farraday clan was cursed after all.

While his flint-like gaze swerved to a white-faced Lucy, who was surrounded by her family and Cole's married sister Penny, a feeling of rage swept through him.

After watching his youngest brother's body being lowered into the ground earlier in the day, he'd been so full of pain he hadn't thought there could be room for any other emotion.

"Thanks, Janine."

The guests were congregated in groups, among them his attorney Jim Darger and his wife. On one side of the room John and Cole's brother-in-law Rich had their heads bent together in serious conversation. On the other, he observed Brenda, a woman he'd been seeing lately, talking with a group of friends. His nieces and nephews had long since disappeared, making him wish he could have joined them.

Under the circumstances no one would notice if he headed for the nearest exit and slipped from the room. The less anyone in the family knew about this the better.

If the intruder in question was enjoying a tour of the place, like some stalking voyeur, his ranch manager Mack would quickly catch up with her.

Acting on a hunch, he let himself out of the house through the study doors and started walking toward the vehicles parked out front. In case she made a dash for one of them, he'd be waiting for her.

To his shock, a woman answering Janine's description got out of a white compact car and called to him in a slightly husky voice. "Excuse me?"

His jaw tightened.

She wasn't at all what he'd anticipated. For one thing she couldn't be in her thirties. For another, her suit was a pale lemon color, subtle and sophisticated. Her healthy, natural ash blond hair didn't look anything close to the cheap image that had filled his mind.

With or without clothes on her slender yet rounded body, there was an elegance to her bones. Those long legs enabled her brilliant blue eyes to meet his without difficulty, and he was a tall man.

Her upswept hair caught in a loose knot revealed classic facial features that needed no enhancement flushed from the heat. He saw intelligence in her glance. More disconcerting to him was the passionate flare of her mouth, as if she could read his mind and enjoyed confounding him. But of course she didn't have the power to do that.

He made the mistake of drawing too close to her. The combination of her own feminine scent and the fragrance either from her hair or perfume, or both, assailed him. Cole hadn't thought anything could drown out the cloying scent of lilies coming from the funeral sprays.

"What can I do for you?" he asked, congratulating himself for sounding willing to help her without revealing the full state of his churning emotions thrown by her presence. But the fact that he had an inordinate curiosity about her proved to be the cause of a deeper irritation at his own undisciplined thoughts on this black day.

"I came to talk to the person who does the hiring on the ranch, but I'm afraid I arrived at an inopportune time. Did someone just get married?"

At the thought of his recently reformed brother gone from this world, leaving Lucy and the whole family in despair, a fresh shaft of pain, sharp and swift, pierced his gut. He rocked back on his hand-tooled cowboy boots. "There was a funeral today."

She bit her lower lip, drawing his attention to that succulent part of her mouth despite his darkest thoughts. What in hell was the matter with him? There'd been women since Jenny died, but none of them had stirred him the way this stranger did. It made no sense.

"Then I'm glad I didn't intrude. Thank you for talking to me." Summarily dismissing him, an experience he couldn't remember ever happening before, she climbed back in her car. In a few seconds she'd be gone.

The sensible part of him wished he could allow her to drive away, but he wasn't finished with her. She'd claimed she wanted to talk to the person in charge of personnel. He did the hiring himself. No one worked at the Bonnibelle—either in the house or on the spread—unless he okayed it.

Whatever the qualifications she might bring for a position she wanted, she'd be the last person he'd consider. Not even then...

She didn't come off flirtatious, which was a surprise. Yet her unconscious sensuality would play havoc with the harmony he'd worked like the devil to maintain among the stockmen since their parents' death in a light airplane crash three years back. Buck had fallen apart after that. It had taken Lucy's sure, steady love for him to start putting himself back together.

Exhaling heavily, Cole took the few steps necessary to place his body next to the door she'd just closed. He braced his hands against the open window and lowered his head.

She turned a surprised gaze to him, giving him the full benefit of her dark fringed eyes, an unusual combination on a blond. A man could think he was falling through a cloudless western sky just looking into them.

"I'm in a position to know there are no job openings, Ms....?"

"Catherine Arnold," she supplied evenly. "Then I should consider myself fortunate I already have a job I love," came the evasive comment.

"I meant no offense."

"None was taken."

Her guileless response disarmed him. She had a lot of ready answers without asking the right questions. There was a reason she'd come to the ranch, but she didn't intend to tell him any more than she had to. That was too bad, because he was determined to learn the truth one way or the other.

"The maid thought you had followed her into the house. When she couldn't find you, she called Security."

Though her expression didn't change, he watched in fascination the way her slim fingers tightened around the steering wheel. She wore no rings, only a gold wristwatch. A clear polish covered her manicured nails. He could see the half-moons of her cuticles clearly.

Everything about her appealed to his senses. That was another thing that hadn't happened to him in years.

A trace of a smile formed on her lips. "And here I was hoping someone would come outside to enlighten me, Mr....?"

"Farraday, but I answer to Cole."

"Thanks for your help, Cole," she said, without as much as a flicker of those long lashes.

Cole wasn't a vain man, but it was a fact that their family's name figured prominently in the settling of this part of Nevada. If she recognized it and was playing dumb, she was a superb actress, particularly since Buck's death had been highly publicized in the media.

Angry at himself for letting her get to him, his chiseled features formed a grimace. "Why do you want to speak to the man who does the hiring?"

"That's my business, surely. No offense," she added in a pleasant tone.

"None taken," came his superficially calm response. "Only I'll have to ask you to step out of the car and accompany me to the owner's office." He'd give her one final chance to own up.

"Why?"

Cole sucked in his breath. Evidently she'd decided not to take it, which could mean she really didn't know who he was. Then again…

"Let's just say it's my job. From here on out you'll have to answer to him." He opened the door, relishing the moment when he exposed her little game, whatever it was.

Her lissom body stiffened. "This is ridiculous. I haven't done anything wrong."

He elevated his dark brows. "Look at it from his point of view. He buried his youngest brother today and came back to the ranch house to be with his closest friends and family. In the process of trying to give comfort to his bereaved sister-in-law, a perfect stranger walks in from out of nowhere with an agenda she refuses to reveal."

While he'd been talking, he didn't think she could fake the growing concern on her face, most likely for the trouble she could be in.

She stirred restlessly. "Doesn't the fact that I called out to you for information prove I have no evil intentions?" The straightforward hint of pleading in her voice almost convinced him.

"On the contrary," he rejoindered coolly, "your behavior is more suspect than ever. Shall we go quietly, or do I take you inside in a manner guaranteed to embarrass you in front anyone who might see you?"

Her face filled with color. "You wouldn't—" she whispered.

Not today, no… He'd find another method. But she didn't know that.

"Try me, Ms. Arnold." He checked his watch. "I'll give you thirty seconds to make up your mind."

CHAPTER TWO

CATHERINE didn't dare call his bluff, not with those cold pewter eyes bearing down on her features, pinning her to the seat.

Standing easily at six-three or four, this powerful-looking security guard, wearing an expensive looking formal suit of midnight-blue in deference to the funeral proceedings, had the hard-muscled physique of a male at home in the out-of-doors.

He was probably in his mid-thirties. She had to admit, albeit begrudgingly, that with his black hair and burnished skin he resembled a rugged facsimile of Adonis. To her ear the name Cole sounded too western for a man who exuded an almost international sophistication.

Having worked the front desk on the night shift at one of Reno's top hotels while she'd finished college, she'd met attractive, wealthy men from all over the world. But if she had to pick just one who was the most memorable, he still wouldn't measure up to the force standing next to her.

That was what this man was—a dynamic, living, breathing force. He radiated a potent male energy that set him apart from those less endowed. She had to concede she'd more than met her match here. If she could appeal to his honor—

Catherine sensed something that told her he was a highly principled male with a superior intellect who probably demanded more discipline from himself than those around him.

How she knew that she couldn't explain, but she recognized that the owner of the ranch had known what he was doing when he'd hired Cole Farraday. She was left with little choice but to reveal what he'd immediately perceived was her secret motive for coming here.

"All right," she exclaimed with a resigned sigh, feeling more vulnerable than ever with the door still open so he could view every inch of her body, which he'd been doing. But in case someone came outside to get in their car, she didn't want to attract attention by standing next to hers in the presence of the security guard.

At least sitting here in the driver's seat, people would think they were simply chatting. Heavens—there was no acceptable way out of this except to get it over with as quickly as possible.

"The truth is, I'm searching for someone."

He kept a hand on top of the open door, perpetuating the fiction that they were acquaintances brought together by the death of a friend. She noted inconsequentially he wore no rings, but that didn't mean he wasn't married. Not that it mattered. She was here for Bonnie's sake, and ultimately for her own.

"That's a start. Man or woman?"

Without looking at him she said, "I've been given reason to believe he might be working on this ranch, or maybe he used to work here."

"Your lover?" he insinuated. "A disgruntled fiancé, perhaps?"

"Neither one," she said, refusing to rise to the bait. But on second thought—considering the circumstances—he'd posed some logical questions. She decided it was his blunt way of speaking that led her to believe he was goading her. After all, the man was only doing his job.

She heard his intake of breath, harsh and distinct. He was growing impatient. "Why do you want to find him?"

The operative question.

Catherine could be blunt too. "To let this man know the teenager he got pregnant gave birth to his baby."

"Ah. That's a very sad story," he answered, with an element

of sincerity she didn't doubt, "but, cruel as this will sound, he probably doesn't want to be found."

"You're right," she agreed in a less than steady voice now. "They never do. The story gets even sadder. The mother, Terrie, died from complications, leaving the baby without a mother or father."

In the periphery she could see the rise and fall of his broad chest. After a tension-filled pause, "This teenager wouldn't be your sister by any chance?"

After her emotional gaffe, he'd made another logical assumption, one that happened to strike too close to home. He couldn't know that despite the difference in their ages, she and Terrie had bonded much like two siblings because of similar life experiences growing up.

Summoning her resolve to hold on to some vestige of control, she said, "No. She's no relation."

"A friend, then?"

She grasped on that. "Yes—" It was the truth, after all, but she was already growing too emotional and he sensed it.

"I noticed from the rim of your license plate you bought this car in Reno. Is that where you live?"

The man's radar didn't miss anything. Whether she chose to tell him or not, he'd be able to find out the pertinent details about her with one simple phone call to the authorities. Considering the nature of his job on such a renowned ranch, the man probably had an inside track. Since he would have friends in high places, she'd save him the trouble.

"Yes."

"Did the teenager in question give birth there too?"

"Yes."

He shifted his weight, an ominous sign which could mean any number of unpleasant things. "Does this cowboy have a name?"

She craned her head in order to look at his brooding features.

"I think he probably made it up so Terrie would never know who he really was for fear she'd try to trace him."

"Out with it, Ms. Arnold." He'd come to the end of his tolerance for what had turned out to be a fencing match. In truth she was tired of dancing around the subject too.

"If I tell you, and you recognize it, you have to promise me you won't reveal it to anyone else—" she cried, then moaned inwardly, wishing she hadn't sounded like she was begging.

"Why do I get the feeling you're trying to protect *him?*" came the silky question.

Her jaw clenched. "I have no love for this man, believe me. But even he has rights I have to honor."

He studied her as if she were a paradox. "In that case, why bother to look him up at all?"

"Because I promised Terrie I would. All she wanted was for him to know he had a daughter. What he does with that information is up to him." Catherine had no doubts he'd do nothing with it. That was what she was counting on. "It's no one else's business."

"What about you?" he questioned.

"I don't understand," she dissembled, vying for time, though she didn't know why because no one was going to come and rescue her from this precarious dilemma.

"Let's not play games." His lips broke into a forbidding curl. "In my gut I know there's a lot more at stake here than your being the simple bearer of this kind of news."

Catherine couldn't afford to lose her cool now. Not in front of this all-seeing, all-knowing watchdog who was sounding much more like a chief prosecutor. She needed to stay calm and collected, like the professional she purported to be.

Filling her lungs with air, she said, "I'm here because of Bonnie."

Though his expression didn't change, a silver flash coming from those suspicious gray eyes indicated she'd hit some kind of nerve. "Bonnie…" he repeated quietly. For want of a more precise word, he sounded haunted.

"Yes. That's the name Terrie gave her baby."

After an almost eerie interim of silence his deep voice spoke again, this time in a gravelly tone. "And the father's name?"

"I-it's one of those nicknames that could belong to any number of men or their horses, especially those living in this part of the country."

"I'm still waiting." He was about to take the action he'd threatened. A small shiver ran down her spine. She was going to have to trust him.

"Terrie said he called himself...Buck."

The second the name left her lips a daunting stillness pervaded the atmosphere. While she could feel the adrenaline driving the speed of her heart, her interrogator carefully shut the door, as if he'd come to some monumental decision.

But when he finally spoke through the open window, the last thing she'd expected to hear was, "Start your car, Ms. Arnold. You're going back to Elko. I'll be right behind you. When we reach the first exit, follow me into town."

So he *did* know Buck and had decided to take her to him.

Catherine experienced a moment of triumph to realize she'd be able to fulfill one of Terrie's dying wishes. For herself she'd been waiting months to confront the amoral male who'd taken advantage of Terrie's youth and naïveté, then discarded her so cruelly, never worrying if there'd be consequences.

"I'll see you there, then," she responded quietly.

With a mixed sense of anxiety and anticipation over what she would learn, Catherine turned on the motor, willing to cooperate with this enigmatic man who held the keys to Buck's whereabouts.

Once she'd made contact, and had satisfied herself he couldn't care less how many children he might have spawned in his selfish need for gratification, she'd be able to carry out Terrie's other wish.

A wish that had become Catherine's *raison d'être*.

Evening had come to the Rubies, prompting Cole to turn on his headlights. The woman at the wheel in front of his power wagon drove at a fast clip, forcing him to concentrate while he made a couple of phone calls, the last one being to his brother.

"John? Hold down the fort, will you? I'm on my way to Elko to take care of some important business."

"I saw you leave a little while ago. Anything I can do to help?"

Cole's thirty-two-year-old married brother was a rock he could always lean on in an emergency. They'd shared pretty much everything in life, but not this time. Not until Cole knew if their little brother had truly fathered a child.

"I'll tell you about it later."

He could hear the question John didn't ask. That was what made him the good man he was.

"When will you be back?"

"I'm not sure."

"Fair enough. Brenda's waiting for you. She's going to be disappointed when I tell her business called you away."

Business, hell—

Cole rubbed his jaw. Brenda was attractive, and he enjoyed her company, but that was all. Unfortunately she wanted more. This was as good a time as any to end it with her. She would have to understand he needed his space to mourn Buck. If she didn't, then he couldn't do anything about it. Catherine Arnold's bombshell had blown him from the path where he'd been letting his life drift. But no longer.

"I'll call her later." He rang off, his thoughts already concentrated on the female who'd managed to get beneath his skin long before he'd learned her visit had anything to do with Buck.

When she took the first turnoff, he sped ahead of her and drove on to the Midas Inn, located in the center of town. Pulling around the side to a private entrance, he jumped down from the cab to help her from the car she'd parked alongside his truck.

Her long, elegant legs distracted him as she got out of the car. "Is this where we're meeting Buck?"

"No." With that one word he'd extinguished the hope in those fabulous blue eyes. "We need to talk. The Midas is one of the ranch owner's investments," he explained, aware of her questioning glance as he pulled her overnight bag from the backseat. "I phoned ahead to arrange a room for you. If you made a reservation somewhere else, let me know and I'll cancel it."

"It's at the Ruby Inn."

"In your own name?"

"Yes," she answered tentatively. "Why do you ask?"

"You come off sounding like you might be an attorney. If so, you could have made your reservation in the name of the firm you work for."

"I'm a social worker at a facility for young single mothers, but I'm not here in an official capacity. My reason for coming is strictly personal, if it's any comfort."

It wasn't.

Buck had shown poor judgment in a lot of cases—but getting involved with an underage girl while he'd been working on their uncle's stud farm outside Reno last summer?

"Maybe that explains why you exhibit the instincts of a clever PI."

"Not that clever, apparently, but I'm not going to complain if it means you can lead me to Bonnie's biological father."

He ushered her inside the building as far as the door of the manager's office. "Follow this hallway to the front desk and give the night clerk your name. He'll take care of you. After you've freshened up, meet me in here."

"Thank you." She managed to get the words out before taking the bag from him. "I won't be long."

"In that case I'll ask the restaurant to bring us a sandwich."

Cole doubted he'd able to eat, but he preferred she didn't suspect he felt like he'd been trampled in a wild mustang stampede no one had seen coming seconds before it happened.

CHAPTER THREE

TEN minutes later Catherine knocked on the manager's door.

"Come in."

Recognizing Cole's deep voice, she walked inside the office. The sight of him standing behind the desk, in a beautiful white dress shirt with the sleeves pushed up his tanned arms to the elbows, rocked her to the foundations.

Minus his tie and suit jacket—the outer trappings of civilized society—his virility was even more in evidence.

By comparison she knew she looked washed out. Other than pulling her hair back in a ponytail, she still wore the suit she'd arrived in. Until she saw the club sandwiches and sliced melon placed on the desk in front of him, she hadn't realized how hungry she was.

"Sit down, Catherine."

The use of her first name indicated progress. Despite their precarious beginning, she liked the sound of it on his lips. She liked the play of muscle across his shoulders and arms. Too much.

Murmuring her assent, she pulled up a chair. Now that the fencing was over, they could get down to business.

He pushed one of the plates toward her, no doubt recognizing the signs of someone who was starving. She reached for a sandwich half and began devouring it. Cole, on the other hand, drank cola from the can while he watched her through shuttered eyes.

Anticipating her needs, he handed her a cola, which she gratefully accepted. She drank most of it before putting the can back on the desk.

"Thank you. I needed that," she exclaimed, glancing at the food he hadn't touched. "Aren't you going to eat?"

"Later. For now I want to hear the details about Terrie and her relationship with Buck." His probing gray eyes were like an assault on her senses. "When they first met—where—how long it lasted—how and when you came into the picture—"

On the drive back to Elko she'd determined to tell him everything she knew in the hope her candor would be rewarded.

"A year ago this month Terrie ran away from her foster home in California. She had the help of another runaway. They stole money and a car. En route they ditched it and stole a van. Once they arrived in Reno, they changed the plates and lived out of it while they washed dishes for a local café called the One-Eyed Jack. On their breaks, they were given free meals."

His brows furrowed. "Resourceful girls."

"The street-smart ones are. They'd been there a month when this 'hunky cowboy'—Terrie's words—showed up and took an immediate interest in her. In fairness to him, she could make herself up to look closer to twenty. He could be excused for not knowing she was only seventeen. After she got off work he would take her dancing, spend money on her. He told her she was beautiful, which she was," Catherine added in an unsteady voice. A brunette with hazel eyes…

Bonnie had been born with a head of dark hair and a rosebud mouth. The sweetest, dearest little baby on earth.

Clearing her throat, Catherine continued. "Soon Terrie was sleeping with him. She didn't have the experience to realize it couldn't last, let alone turn into anything permanent like a wedding ring on her finger. By September he was gone from her life without a trace, leaving her pregnant and ill with morning sickness. The café manager had to let her go, but she gave Terrie the name of a home run by private donations called Girls' Haven."

"You're the case worker there?" He sat back in the chair with his strong arms folded.

"Yes. I've been working there for three years. Stories like Terrie's are all too common. Her friend dropped her off in the van, then drove away. Terrie never saw her or Buck again."

"Did this Buck actually tell her he worked on the Bonnibelle?"

"He didn't tell her anything concrete about his life except that he was a cowboy. The night before he disappeared, someone came in the café looking for him while he was waiting for her to go off shift. She overheard this person tell Buck he'd better call the Bonnibelle on the double. Terrie went through her pregnancy assuming the other man had been referring to a woman Buck hadn't told her about, and that's why he'd abandoned her. It wasn't until she was dying from an infection following the delivery that she broke down and told me about the incident. That's when I told her Bonnibelle was the name of a famous ranch somewhere in Nevada."

Their eyes held for a brief moment, sending an errant thrill through her body that had nothing to do with business.

"At that point Terrie said she wanted the name Bonnie put on the birth certificate. She begged me to find Buck so he'd know he had a daughter."

Maybe it was the dim light of the office, but lines of what could be interpreted as exasperation mixed with sorrow gave Cole's hard-boned face an almost haggard appearance. She had to remember he'd attended a funeral earlier in the day. The mention of Terrie's death must have triggered emotions still close to the surface.

Catherine could relate. She was still in pain and shock that the teen she'd grown so close to in the last year was gone, and wouldn't be able to raise her little girl. Life could be cruelly unfair to some people—

"What's the name of the hospital where she delivered?"

"Reno Regional." Her voice caught.

"When was the birth?"

"June twentieth."

"Five weeks old already?" He echoed her concern.

She nodded.

"The only reason she hasn't been adopted yet is because she was born five weeks premature. For a while she was on a ventilator and had to be fed through an IV. They had to recreate conditions in the womb. She also had a bad case of jaundice and had to be placed under lights."

Catherine had spent every possible minute with Bonnie after work and on weekends, touching her through the holes of the hospital incubator until she could hold her and feed her the special formula. She couldn't love her more if she'd given birth from her own body.

"Where's the baby now?"

"In a temporary foster home awaiting adoption." That familiar jabbing pain tore at her heart. "A newborn baby is in such high demand, Bonnie will probably find a permanent home with an adoptive family within the next week. That's why it's necessary I speak to Buck right away."

"Provided he's the father," his voice grated.

"A DNA test will put the matter to rest one way or the other," she reminded him, though of course he didn't need to be told that. "The hospital already has the results on Bonnie. It's a routine procedure for prospective adoptees."

Cole rubbed the back of his bronzed neck. She had the further impression he was near exhaustion, unknowingly soliciting her sympathy. Whoever had died must have been a close friend.

A strange sound escaped his throat before he sat forward in the swivel chair. "I'll arrange for Buck's DNA to be sent for comparison."

"Can you ask them to put a rush on it?" She knew he had the clout to light fires.

"I'm as anxious to clear this up as you are," he ground out. "What was Terrie's last name?"

"She went by Cloward with a C. That's on her records both

at Girls' Haven and the hospital. But I'm sure she made it up, since she told the café manager it was Markham. No doubt Terrie told Buck something altogether different. They both had their secrets," she lamented, surprising a troubling bleakness coming from his eyes.

"In case he pretends not to recognize her description, I have a photograph you can give him. It was taken before she was showing. In this one she's not wearing makeup or clothes that tend to make her look older."

She pulled it from her purse and handed it to Cole, who studied Catherine intently several seconds before looking at it.

"You're right," he eventually murmured. "She's attractive in the way a girl is who's standing on the brink of womanhood."

Despite Terrie's history, Catherine could tell Cole could see what Catherine had seen in her...a young, troubled teen in need of help. A girl much like Catherine had been once upon a time. The knowledge caused her to warm to him unexpectedly.

"Buck's charm managed to turn her into one." Catherine tried to keep the bitterness out of her voice, but failed. "She said he was her first experience, and that it was wonderful. *He* was wonderful. Tender. Again, those were Terrie's words. I—I have to admit I was glad for that at least," she stammered.

"You believed her?"

"Yes." She drew in a quick breath. "Terrie had no reason to lie about him. Not after admitting to breaking several laws. But it doesn't really matter. The fact is, she loved him and died of a broken heart long before the infection became impossible to stop."

Reaching in her purse, she pulled out more photos. "These show Bonnie in the premie ICU, hooked up to all those tubes."

He reached for them.

"Newborn pictures never do a baby justice, especially when

they have as hard a time as Bonnie. You can see her swollen eye and how yellow she is there, poor darling."

Silence filled the office while Cole took his time studying them.

"Here's one I took of her two days ago. If this is any indication, she's going to be a real beauty like her mother."

While he examined it she said, "Am I allowed to ask a question now?"

Slowly he lifted his dark head. "Go ahead." His voice grated.

"What's his marital status?"

His face closed up. "He was married two months ago."

"That news would have killed Terrie," she whispered. "Assuming he *is* Bonnie's father, I can't imagine him wanting to claim her now. But on the outside chance that there's a part of him wanting to do the right thing, then I—"

Before she could finish the rest of her sentence, Cole was on his feet, stunning her with the speed that had propelled his powerful body out of the chair.

"I have something to do before any more time passes." He reached for his suit jacket, where he pocketed the photos. "I'll call you in Reno tomorrow," he said, grabbing for his tie. "Give me your cellphone number."

She wrote it on her business card and handed it to him.

He came around the desk and accompanied her to the door, moving with that careless male grace that distinguished him from other men. Like a wall of heat, she felt the sweep of those silvery flecked eyes.

"Your bill's been taken care of. Have a good sleep and a safe trip home, Catherine."

"Bonnie had her mid-morning bottle but she still fussed before going to sleep. She gets all excited when you come, and misses you when you're not here. It's amazing!"

Uh-oh.

"What's her schedule like?"

"She's eating every three hours."

I know. I was there from the beginning.

Catherine had just driven in from Elko. Normally she would have gone to her condo and showered before starting her work day. But she hadn't seen Bonnie for twenty-four hours. Driving to the ranch and back had made it feel like she'd been gone a week. Babies changed every day. She envied Carol Wilson for being able to take care of her on a round-the-clock basis.

Unable to restrain herself, she kissed the baby's cheeks several times before raising up. "She looks contented now. I'll be by again tomorrow, Carol."

The best part of Catherine's job was to visit the foster parents and check on the babies. But her pleasure had become pain because Bonnie didn't belong to her.

Assuming Buck was the father, and he wanted his daughter, then they had the God-given right to be with each other and Catherine would have to find a way to live with it.

But if he gave up all parental rights to her...

"She's a sweetie pie," Carol said, walking Catherine to the front door. "Makes me baby-hungry again, but Phil says three children are enough." She winked. "Between you and me, this one's going to be hard to give up. I swear I couldn't do your job or I'd want to take every baby home with me."

Catherine murmured something appropriate and hurried out to her car. The last thing she wanted was for Carol to witness her emotional turmoil. Already she was wondering how she would make it through the day while she waited for Cole Farraday's phone call.

She had an idea the man could move mountains. When he called, he would have news for her, and he'd deliver it in that deep, cultured voice. Anticipating even talking to him again made her feel breathless.

CHAPTER FOUR

As it turned out, she didn't hear from him until she got home from work at six-thirty that evening. She'd just stepped out of the shower and changed into a T-shirt and jeans when her cellphone rang. The caller ID indicated out of area, which might or might not be the call she'd been waiting for all day.

She clicked on, aware her pulse was racing. "This is Catherine Arnold."

After a pause, "You do realize that in answering the way you do, you give any crazy out there more information than you might want him to know."

Her hand tightened around the phone while a fire and ice sensation spread through her body. It was a little like eating crème de menthe on top of vanilla ice cream.

In truth no man had ever shown her this kind of concern before. She was so used to fending for herself. Cole Farraday's unexpected comment reminded her he was that exceptional kind of male who would protect his own to the death.

What would it feel like to be loved and taken care of by a man like that for the rest of your life? Catherine couldn't comprehend it any more than she could imagine what it would be like to have a mother and father, or siblings.

"You're right, but since a lot of troubled teens phone me when they're most vulnerable or desperate, I want them to know they don't have to go through a third party to find me."

"Point taken, Catherine. No offense," he murmured.

She sank down on the edge of her bed, attacked by a sudden weakness. "None taken."

"Are you still at work?"

"No. I—I'm home." Her voice faltered.

"Alone?"

Did he ask that question because he wanted to keep their conversation private, or was she hoping something of a more personal nature was behind it?

"Yes," she said quietly. "Do you have news for me yet?"

"I do, but I need to see you in person."

So the Buck he knew *was* Bonnie's father! Otherwise he would have told her there was no DNA match and she could check at the hospital for the results herself.

Did it mean Buck wanted to see his daughter?

Torn by conflicting emotions, she jumped to her feet. "When can you be in Reno?"

"I flew in this morning."

Her heart leaped. He'd been here all day? Now she wouldn't have to wait until tomorrow. "Where are you?"

"I'm just leaving the hospital. For the sake of everyone concerned I'd prefer to meet you in private."

Catherine felt the same way. After pressing her lips together she said, "Come to my condo. I'm in a fourplex southeast of the hospital." She gave him the address and instructions to get there. "It's a little complicated."

"I'll find you."

She had no doubt of it.

With a fluttery feeling in her chest, she clicked off before racing back to the bathroom to fix her freshly washed hair and change into a cotton shirt.

Cole's first thought when he walked into her cozy living room was that she was even more beautiful than he remembered from the night before. The dusky rose of her top, pulled down over white pants covering womanly hips, blended with the blush of her complexion.

Like a gossamer curtain, she'd allowed her hair to fall loose from a side part. It swished against her shoulders with each step she took.

Following the long line of her shapely legs to sandaled feet, he could find no flaw in the way she was put together, let alone her color scheme.

"Won't you sit down?" She indicated the couch opposite the chair she'd claimed, ensuring some distance between them. Cole had the distinct feeling the awareness between them was growing stronger for her too.

Though she presented a poised, professional attitude, he sensed a barely suppressed anxiety coming from her, apart from her eagerness to get straight to the point.

She couldn't afford to get this involved with every case, otherwise she'd burn out from the intensity. If she'd spent a lot of time in the premie nursery with the baby, it would explain why she'd become so emotionally attached.

It was a situation beyond the norm—an occasional hazard in her line of work, he surmised. She'd said her visit to the ranch was unofficial.

Who would have imagined his brother being at the core of Terrie Cloward's heartbreak and ultimate demise?

"Buck's the father, isn't he?" The question brought him back to the source of his bone-deep sorrow with a jolt.

"Yes. His paternity's not in question."

She sat forward. "Did he fly here with you?"

Cole detected a distinct throb in her voice. Her behavior was all the more intriguing in spite of his pain. "No. His DNA results were faxed from the hospital in Elko."

She stood up, evidently too restless to stay seated. "Does that mean he didn't want anything to do with Bonnie, even when he discovered he had a daughter?" she cried.

Something earthshaking was going on inside her to lose control like that. Join the club. Dear God.

How in the hell would Buck have responded upon learning he was a father? Poor Lucy... Still in the honeymoon stage, who could say how she would have handled the shock? With news of that nature even the strongest marriage would be tested to the ultimate degree.

The questions bombarded him, bringing him to his feet. "Since I can't speak for him," he began solemnly, "I can't honestly answer you."

Catherine faced him with an incredulous look. "What do you mean, can't? Surely when you told him he needed to go to the hospital to have the DNA test done, he knew exactly why?"

He massaged the tight cords at the back of his neck. There was something he needed to do before this went any further.

"I'd like to see the baby, then I'll answer all your questions."

She searched his eyes in bewilderment before shaking her head. "My hands are legally tied. Only the father can have access, or, in the unlikely case of his death, his next of kin."

Cole inhaled sharply. "You're looking at him."

A myriad of emotions chased over her face until comprehension dawned. Then she gasped softly. "The funeral—"

He gave an almost imperceptible nod of his head. "My youngest brother, Patrick Farraday. Killed in a riding accident out on the range last week. Our father called him Buck at an early age and it stuck."

She clung to the back of the chair. "But you said it was the *owner* of the Bonnibelle who—"

He wasn't destined to hear more, because a moan had escaped her throat, preventing the rest from coming out. She'd finally put the pieces together.

"Until his recent reformation, my little brother didn't always do the right thing—as you've already discovered. But for all his faults and virtues, he was my brother and I loved him."

Her eyes grew suspiciously bright. "Naturally you wanted to protect him. You did a superb job of it, Mr. Farraday."

"So did you," he riposted. "Another person in your official capacity might have taken it into her head to expose some of the family secrets last evening, damaging Buck's fragile widow."

She searched his eyes. "They'd only been married two months?"

"That's right. After working on a relative's stud farm outside Reno part of last summer, I told him he was needed at home. To my surprise he actually showed up without an argument. When he arrived he declared his partying days were over. Evidently something had happened to make him realize he'd been going in the wrong direction."

His eyes caught hers. "Now we know what it was. In one of his sober moments, he must have realized his mistake in getting involved with someone as young as Terrie. At least I'd like to think so. A couple of months later he announced his engagement to Lucy, the girl who'd been crazy about him for years."

Catherine rubbed her arms. "How old was Buck?"

"Thirty last birthday."

"It's too tragic," she whispered.

He nodded. "A double tragedy considering Terrie died so recently. I'd like to see Bonnie tonight."

His request seemed to startle her. "It's too late to make arrangements with her foster family. But, more to the point, it's my professional opinion it wouldn't be a good idea."

Cole shifted his weight. "Good idea be damned. She's a Farraday. She has a birthright she shares with uncles, aunts and cousins."

Catherine studied him through veiled eyes. "Nevertheless, you're grieving the loss of your brother. You don't need this to compound it, not when she's going to be adopted. It would be better not to put yourself in a position where you could form an attachment."

His teeth ground together. "Simply knowing I have a niece,

I already feel attached to her. You gave me pictures of her I'm not likely to forget, remember?" he challenged.

She stiffened. "At the time I didn't realize you were her uncle."

He stifled an oath. "Without proof from the DNA, neither did I."

"Look, Mr. Farraday—" She spread her hands in a conciliatory gesture. "Let's not make this any harder than it is. Terrie asked me to find Buck. I've honored her wishes, and my heart goes out to you and your family. But the reality is, Bonnie's a ward of the court. A judge will decide her new home."

He had to tamp down his temper. "It will never take the place of that spot of earth her ancestors settled and gave their life's blood for."

"But would it be her home if Terrie hadn't died?" She held her ground with surprising tenacity. "Do you honestly believe your married brother would have wanted visitation rights?"

From the first Cole had been asking himself that question. "The reformed Buck would have," he theorized. "But since both parents are gone the point is moot. It's a new playing field."

"You're right. And that playing field has to serve Bonnie's best interests. Do you have any idea how many people incapable of having children are dying for a baby like her to love and raise?" Her voice trembled. "Some have been preparing years for the privilege."

From the raw emotion she exuded, he could almost believe she was talking about herself. If she'd been at Girls' Haven three years, she undoubtedly grew close to the teens who found themselves in trouble. It wasn't that different from him getting to know the stockmen who worked for him. At times their problems became his.

Terrie's death had to have been hard on her, not to mention Bonnie's hospital stay. Much as he hated this situation, Cole admired her wisdom and dedication to the job. On top of everything else, she'd shown discretion, a noble attribute when all was said and done.

Changing tactics, he said, "I only want to see her. Will you arrange it for me?" He could call his attorney to do it for him, but, for several reasons he hadn't examined too closely yet, Cole preferred to deal with her alone.

She let out a sigh that sounded troubled, if not anguished. "How long will you be in Reno?"

"For as long as it takes."

A battle seemed to be going on inside her. After a tension-filled silence her gaze fell away and she gave a brief nod. "Come by at nine in the morning and she'll be here."

Without further word she walked to the door, indicating it was time for him to leave. No woman of his acquaintance had ever done that to him before. Contrarily, he didn't want to go. There was a lot more he wanted to know about her.

She didn't wear a wedding ring. As far as he could tell she wasn't living with another man. He saw no signs of a male occupying her home, but that didn't mean there wasn't one in the picture. A woman who looked and moved like her would attract them in droves.

Hell—he'd been drawn to her from the moment her husky voice had called out to him yesterday. Being with her tonight, those feelings had only intensified.

He moved toward her. "I'll get out of here so whoever you're expecting won't jump to a hasty conclusion."

"Thank you, Mr. Farraday." Ignoring his gambit, she opened the door. But satisfying color swept into her cheeks, intensifying the electric blue of those fabulous eyes, giving him the answer he sought. For the moment anyway.

"I'll be here on the dot of nine," he assured her before walking toward his rental car.

No sooner had he driven away than he pulled out his phone to check his messages. He'd turned off the ringer so he wouldn't be disturbed while he talked to Catherine.

Two were from Brenda, the others from John and Penny. If he'd seen one from Mack, then he would have known something was wrong at the ranch.

Under the circumstances he didn't feel like talking to anyone. From the second he'd taken a look at Bonnie's pictures an idea had been percolating in his brain. After talking to Catherine this evening, it had taken on critical mass.

CHAPTER FIVE

CATHERINE brought the baby into the living room. "When I picked her up this morning, she'd just finished her bottle. I'm afraid she's about to fall asleep again."

Their eyes met for a moment. Cole's were alive with anticipation. "No problem."

As if he were used to taking care of an infant, he plucked Bonnie from her arms and carried her across the expanse to the sofa.

Such a tiny bundle nestled securely against the broad shoulder of a powerfully built man like Cole caught at Catherine's heart. She heard low, happy laughter rumble out of him as he laid Bonnie on the cushion and began examining her.

Catherine had been guilty of doing the very same thing before he had arrived. Now she was guilty of examining *his* body, dressed in a navy polo shirt and pleated trousers.

Terrie had fallen in love with a "hunky" cowboy named Buck.

Now that Catherine had met his big brother—the dynamic owner and head of the Bonnibelle Ranch—she understood the power of the Farraday charm. It was lethal.

Bonnie must think so too. While she focused on the man speaking to her in that deep, rich voice, giving her all his attention, her whole tiny body seemed to wriggle with new life.

Without conscious thought Catherine drew closer, marveling at certain similarities between the two of them. Though she saw a look of Terrie in Bonnie's mouth and nose, her hair color and widow's peak, the shape of her eyes was genuine Farraday. Was it any wonder she was such a beautiful child?

Cole seemed captivated by her, as if he'd forgotten Catherine was in the room. Pleasure in the baby caused the lines of his face to disappear for a moment, making him look younger and so handsome it hurt.

It was only natural he was thinking of his brother and the little girl he and Terrie had produced. Yet every minute spent with her would make it that much harder for Cole to let her go.

No one understood that better than Catherine herself.

Time was passing. She had to bring this love-fest between uncle and niece to an end.

"Cole?" she called softly to him. "I've bent the rules by bringing Bonnie here. She has an appointment with the pediatrician in a half-hour. Now that you've had the opportunity to see her, I'm afraid we have to leave."

That brought his dark head around. "Is there something still wrong with her?" he demanded quietly.

After the way he'd been playing with the baby, testing the strength of her fingers and kissing her sweet neck, it shouldn't have surprised her he'd reacted to Catherine's words like any typical anxious parent.

"Not at all, otherwise the hospital wouldn't have released her. It's standard procedure that while the babies are in foster care routine checkups are done with more frequency than usual because they can be adopted at any time." She flashed him an apologetic smile. "I don't want to be late."

Actually the doctor would fit the babies' visits in without an appointment, but Cole didn't need to know that.

Perhaps it was an unconscious gesture on his part, but in the next breath he'd laid Bonnie against his shoulder, exhibiting an undeniably possessive hold on her that was at once stunning and touching.

The thing Catherine had hoped wouldn't happen had already come to pass. His next words confirmed it.

"No stranger is going to adopt her. I won't allow it."

Cole Farraday was used to his word being law, but in this case the situation wasn't so black and white. Catherine took a fortifying breath. "Then you'll need to tell that to the judge. I'll warn you now that, even with money and power on your side, he'll want what's best for Bonnie."

"She's going to come home to her rightful family," he declared in a forceful tone.

"Are you married, Cole?"

His jaw hardened. "I'm a widower, but in this day and age having a wife isn't a prerequisite, surely?"

It appeared he'd known a lot of sorrow in his life, but then so had Catherine. She couldn't let sentiment dissuade her from her course.

"Perhaps not always, but there are other considerations."

"What consideration could possibly be more important than the fact that Bonnie is already loved by her own surviving flesh and blood?"

Panicked, Catherine could feel the baby slipping away from her, figuratively as well as physically.

"Terrie left written wishes before she died," Catherine answered him. "They hold weight with the court."

She caught the glint of fire coming from his eyes. "You fulfilled them by driving to the ranch to find Buck." His expression mirrored a faint respect for what she'd done, but that was all.

Her heart kicked against her ribs. "There was another wish."

She could almost feel his arms close tighter around Bonnie. "Am I going to have to pry that out of you too?"

His black brows took on a threatening slant, but she was fighting for her life and refused to be intimidated.

"In the event I couldn't find Buck, Terrie designated someone specific to raise Bonnie."

The sudden indrawn breath she heard sounded like ripping silk.

"Someone waiting in the wings, you mean, yet you wouldn't tell me even if the law didn't forbid you," he reflected bitterly, in what she guessed was a rare show of temper.

In the stillness that followed, he rubbed the back of the baby's head with a tenderness that melted Catherine's insides.

She sensed his frustration. Under other circumstances she'd be on his side all the way. "I'm sorry. As it is I shouldn't have let you come here to see Bonnie."

But he wasn't listening, and she heard his next words delivered with barely veiled hostility. "That explains why you were in such an all-fired hurry to get the DNA match done."

"Cole, I—"

"Obviously it's someone in Terrie's confidence." He continued with his train of thought, staring at her as if he'd suddenly been given second sight. "A woman with a vested interest in her wellbeing and that of her child."

He took a step toward her. "It's *you,* isn't it?"

Catherine started to shake.

"I *knew* there was something different about you, something that didn't quite add up. A social worker's job doesn't include driving across Nevada to find a man who might have impregnated one of the teens at Girls' Haven."

His gunsmoke eyes impaled her. "Now it's making sense. You had to be certain Buck wouldn't claim his rights before you put in your petition to adopt Bonnie yourself."

Catherine could see there was no point in denying it, not when his steel trap mind had figured it out.

He kissed the top of the baby's head. "Terrie may have wanted you to raise her daughter, but, considering your position as the social worker for Girls' Haven, I can guarantee that a judge will see your petition for adoption as a conflict of interest."

"I'm sure he will," she admitted to him. "But the circumstances were extraordinary. I spent five weeks at the hospital with Bonnie, and now she needs me. I'm counting on the judge to weigh the facts that I love this baby with all my heart, and I have Terrie's blessing. Don't make me out to be some kind of monster. Terrie wanted to give Buck the chance to claim Bonnie. So did I," she defended. "Every child deserves its parents if it's humanly possible. The truth is, I was orphaned as a baby, never knowing who mine were. Like Terrie I lived in various foster homes and ended up at Girls' Haven, pregnant at the same age."

His lips thinned, undoubtedly in revulsion.

"Terrie's and my stories are very similar, except that I planned to keep my baby. But it wasn't meant to be because I miscarried at four months. I never got the chance to hold my little girl or love her."

Don't break down now, Catherine.

"But thanks to Girls' Haven I was given a second chance at life and I took it. That was eleven years ago. A lot has happened since then. After university I came to work for them, hoping to give back what they gave me. Getting to know Terrie and her situation was like experiencing *déjà vu*. Over the last months we grew very close," she explained, endeavoring to get through to him. "She always planned to give up her baby for adoption. When she realized she was dying, she begged me to be Bonnie's mother." Her voice shook. "I told her that if I couldn't find Buck, or if he didn't want Bonnie, I—I'd do everything in my power to adopt her."

Catherine had a struggle to hold the tears back. "It wasn't hard to make that promise. She's the most precious, adorable baby on earth."

Though his hand spanned Bonnie's little back lovingly, his eyes still glittered dangerously. "A wise judge will suspect you used your considerable influence to coerce Terrie into putting her wishes in writing."

"A good judge will take the extenuating facts into consideration and rule what's best for Bonnie," she countered, swallowing hard. "In all probability we'll both lose out, and he'll award the adoption to a couple so Bonnie will grow up with a mother *and* father. It's something neither you nor I can provide."

The tension between them sizzled.

"That's unacceptable."

"You think I don't feel the same way?" came her anguished cry.

Catherine understood his anger since she felt defeated by the same ineffectual emotion. This was a situation she would never have envisioned. Not in a lifetime.

"Will you please give Bonnie to me? I have to get her ready to go to the doctor."

She expected another argument, but shockingly he said something quite different in a low aside. "Let me help. Where's her carryall?"

It was in her bedroom, but she didn't want him of all people going in there. "I'll get it."

When she hurried back with it, he lowered Bonnie into it as if he'd done this sort of thing many times before. He'd mentioned having nephews and nieces, so it wasn't surprising he seemed a natural.

As she tucked a receiving blanket around Bonnie, who was being a perfect angel, her arm brushed against Cole's. He didn't act as if he'd noticed, but she felt sudden warmth spiral through her body.

"Come on, sweetheart," she said a bit unsteadily. "It's time to go get checked out."

"I'll carry her out to the car for you."

Catherine didn't say anything because she knew she couldn't stop him. His proprietorial interest in Bonnie was nothing short of astounding.

He must have seen her vehicle out in the carport because he knew exactly where to go.

Amy, the good-looking redheaded Realtor who lived in the next condo, was just walking toward her car. She almost tripped over a crack in the cement while she stared at Cole. As an afterthought she said hello to Catherine, who could read the other woman's mind.

Unfortunately Catherine knew her aggressive neighbor would be over later to find out who the mystery man was, because there was no question about it, Cole Farraday was an incredibly gorgeous man. However, this was one time Catherine didn't intend to satisfy Amy's curiosity.

After she unlocked her car, Cole fastened Bonnie's carryall into the base of the back seat. Through the rearview mirror Catherine watched him kiss the baby's nose and cheeks. His display of affection wasn't feigned. This was his brother's baby and he was crazy about her.

But so was Catherine!

He approached her window, which she had to put down. "What time do you eat lunch?"

His deep voice disturbed her as much as his nearness. She might have known Cole wasn't going to let this go. "Most of the time I don't," she said, playing for time so she could think.

"Then I'll come by Girls' Haven later and we'll talk."

"No!" she cried in panic. "That would be the worst thing you could do." She clung to the steering wheel.

His presence would create a major upheaval, starting with Sylvia, the director, who would ask questions Catherine would be forced to answer. It could get her into serious trouble and he knew it!

A satisfied gleam had entered those silvery eyes. "We have unfinished business, Catherine. You name the place."

"There *is* no place that would be safe for us to be seen together," she confessed.

"My thoughts precisely."

He had the upper hand. If she didn't know better, she would think he was actually enjoying this.

"Meet me here at two. I can spare a half-hour. No more."

Needing to get away from him, she started the car and began to back out. He stood there with his hands on his hips in a totally male stance. After driving away, she could still feel his penetrating eyes following her.

Cole's motive for wanting to see her again was transparent. With family blood on his side, he believed she didn't have a chance of adopting Bonnie. But rather than fight her he intended to use that potent Farraday charm to gain her cooperation in helping him win custody of the baby. He wasn't the head of the Bonnibelle for nothing.

But Catherine didn't plan to make Terrie's mistake and be drawn in by male persuasion at the hands of a master. Watching Cole interact with the baby had given her an idea, one that grew as the day wore on. Under the circumstances it made the most sense.

A few hours later she tried it out on him. For an answer Cole's mocking tone resounded in her living room. "You'll grant *me* liberal visitation rights?"

She'd been five minutes late returning to the condo from her work, and was still out of breath. They faced each other like adversaries.

"Yes. I've been thinking about it since I took the baby back to her foster family. You and I could petition the judge in the same pre-trial hearing. Don't you see it might strengthen both our cases if we show that we're willing to work together for Bonnie's ultimate welfare?"

Cole's mouth compressed. "Who's going to raise her during the day while you're at work?" At least he'd cooled down enough to have a conversation.

She was ready for that question. "Terrie and I talked about it. There's a wonderful daycare facility right across the street from Girls' Haven. I'll be close to her and can oversee everything on a constant basis."

He made a dismissive gesture. "My housekeeper could provide the same care, but I doubt the judge will be impressed with either scenario."

"So what are you saying?" she blurted, trying to tamp down her alarm.

His gaze wandered over her features with a lazy sensuality he probably wasn't aware of. "That your original assumption was correct. The ideal for Bonnie would be to have a stay-at-home mother whose husband provides the necessary income."

His pessimism over her idea of a joint petition acted like a giant hand crushing her heart. If Cole, with all his resources and a last name like his, didn't think they could sway the judge, what chance did she really have to fight for Bonnie on her own?

Tears glazed her eyes before she could turn away. She buried her face in her hands, trying not to make a sound. In searching for Buck, the dream world she'd been living in for the last five weeks had shattered. "No stranger will ever love her as much as I do."

"That makes two of us," he whispered behind her. "I see my brother in her, and it kills me."

The pathos in his voice reached down to the core of her being. Catherine had no more desire to fight him.

She sniffed before wiping her eyes with the back of her hands. "I-if you plan to fight for her, I'll help any way I can. The judge needs to hear how much Terrie loved your brother, and how much you loved him. Just promise me that if you win you'll let me see her once in a while?" her voice throbbed.

"Oh, I plan to win," he finally said in a low, husky tone. "I have an ace up my sleeve guaranteed to produce results."

The hairs prickled on the back of her neck. Catherine turned to him, staring at him through blurry eyes. "What is it?"

"I've decided to get married."

She received the news like a physical blow, but by some miracle she remained standing.

"Th-that ought to do it," she stammered helplessly. "With or without my help."

"I'll need that too, but we'll talk about it this evening over dinner. I'll be by at six."

"I'm afraid I can't tonight. A new case is coming in. I probably won't be leaving the office until nine or nine-thirty." For once she was grateful she had to work late. The bombshell he'd just dropped had disturbed her in ways she didn't dare examine.

"You can ask someone else to cover for you."

"It would have to be an emergency."

"What if I told you it is?"

He sounded deadly serious.

"I don't understand."

"How could you when you don't know all the facts?"

Cole seemed to be talking in riddles.

"Have you arranged to meet with your attorney? Is that why you need me there? So I can give him the relevant details?"

"We'll do that too. But first I've made an appointment with a justice of the peace."

She blinked. "Surely you don't need me to witness your marriage—"

A strange smile broke out on his arresting features. "No. I need you to marry me tonight."

She let out a caustic laugh. "Oh, please—"

"My word exactly," he came back in a frighteningly sober tone. "Following that we'll fill out adoption papers on Bonnie that my attorney will present to the judge. You were the one who warned me time was of the essence."

The world tilted for a moment.

Catherine lost cognizance of time and place, because she knew Cole never said anything he didn't mean, or wasn't prepared to carry out.

"It's the only solution," he added, taking advantage of her silence. "We're both free and we both want to be a parent to Bonnie. As Buck's brother and Terrie's choice of woman to raise her daughter, we can offer something no one else can. There's one caveat, however," he added, sounding mysterious.

She was still too deep in shock to respond, and he knew it.

"When I take you and Bonnie home to the ranch, I'll be introducing you as the woman I fell in love with a year ago. We found out we were expecting a baby, but you refused to marry me because you were afraid I was still too in love with the memory of my deceased wife."

"Are you?" she fired hotly.

"I'll always love Jenny, but she belongs to my past. Unfortunately there are people who for reasons of their own insist on believing otherwise."

"Meaning your ex-girlfriends?"

An amused gleam entered his eyes. "After our daughter was born you realized I really did love you. Hoping it wasn't too late for us, you came to the ranch on the day of Buck's funeral and asked me to marry you. Naturally I was overjoyed and insisted we get married immediately."

Catherine shook her head, finally managing to find her voice. "In the first place, two strangers don't meet one day and get married the next—and even if by the remotest possibility we did, I couldn't live around your family with a lie like that—"

His features hardened. "Then we'll tell the truth in front of everyone, which will include Lucy. She'll learn that Buck got involved with a teenager and the baby is his. That we had to get married in order to adopt her. Lucy will put two and two together, figuring out Bonnie was conceived just weeks before Buck returned to the ranch and asked her to marry him."

"No—" Catherine cried. "That would be too awful, too cruel to her. It could destroy her faith in love. She'd grieve forever."

"Then which is it?" he inserted suavely. "You can't have it both ways if you want to be a mother to Bonnie."

Catherine wanted it more than anything in the world. She'd promised Terrie. But to get married to a man she'd only met two days ago…

What did she really know about him except that he was the owner of the famous Bonnibelle Ranch?

He wants Bonnie as much as you do, her heart reminded her. *He wants you to help him raise his brother's baby. That's what you know about him, deep down in your soul.*

Her body trembled. Was that enough reason to do something so drastic it would change her whole life and his?

"Do you know the odds against a marriage like that working?" she cried.

"Probably as good as the odds of any marriage making it," he countered, with a cynicism she vaguely shared.

"Where would we live?"

"In my house."

"You mean the ranch house?"

"No. My brother and sister and their families live there. Buck lived there with Lucy, but I suspect that one of these days she'll move back to Elko to be near her family. My house is on the other side of the lake."

"Is it where you lived with your wife?"

"No. Like everyone else, Jenny and I began our married life in the ranch house."

Though she hated asking the next question, she had to know. "How did she die?"

"A drunk teenager ploughed into her car one night as she was driving back to the ranch. She died instantly."

Catherine's face crumpled in pain. "I'm so sorry."

She felt his eyes studying her. "After she was gone, I built a place of my own to get away from the memories. My sister Penny jokingly calls it the bachelor pad, but with your help we can make it family-friendly. I dare you to come and live in it with Bonnie and me." He flashed her a rare white smile that turned her heart over.

Shaken by his proposal, she drew in an unsteady breath, attempting to keep her wits. "Supposing I were to say yes to this ludicrous idea of yours, and we get married only to learn that the judge turns down our petition?"

He gave an elegant shrug of those masculine shoulders. "Then we get an annulment. I'll have my attorney put it in writing. But if we win Bonnie, our marriage is forever."

Forever.

She reeled in place.

He paused at the door. "I'll be by at six for your answer. If you're not here, then I'll know she isn't your *raison d'être* after all."

CHAPTER SIX

AT FIVE to six Cole pulled up in front of Catherine's condo. He'd come early because, frankly, there was nowhere else he wanted to be.

Throughout his life he'd relied on gut instinct to get him through some rough moments. By asking him if he would let her visit Bonnie sometimes, she'd admitted defeat. It was the pain he'd heard in Catherine's voice that had made up his mind for him.

Now it was a waiting game to see if she had the courage to do this outrageous thing and marry him.

"Coletrane—" he could hear his father "—whether you like it or not, you're a natural-born leader. I'm depending on you to hold this family together after I'm gone someday. Buck bears watching, and Penny and John will always look to you, whether in good times or bad."

Cole ground his teeth.

Watching Buck self-destruct despite many unsuccessful interventions on Cole's part had turned him inside out. But he could do something for his brother now. He *wanted* to do it.

Already he thought of the baby as *his* little Bonnibelle. She was a fighter to have gotten through those first difficult five weeks. Nothing in life seemed more important than being a father to her. With Catherine helping him, they could be the family Cole ached for and Bonnie deserved.

He checked his watch. Five after six.

His chest grew tight. If he was wrong about Catherine and she couldn't bring herself to marry him, not even for the baby's sake, then he'd call out every favor to influence the judge to let him adopt Bonnie alone.

It might entail an all-out battle with the court. That was okay. He was ready for the fight, even if it meant pretending *he'd* been Terrie's lover. A white lie God would understand. His and Buck's DNA would be a close enough match.

But he much preferred the thought of being Catherine's husband.

Since the idea had come to him, it was all he'd been able to think about. She was a beautiful woman. Her haunting image had played havoc with his sleep. He couldn't forget how careful she'd been to protect Buck, or how brave she'd been to stand up to Cole no matter what he threw at her.

They would have something going for them most newlyweds didn't have—a ready-made child they both loved. In that regard he and Catherine shared an unassailable bond. It was what had brought them together. Who knew what the future might hold for them?

In two days she'd become so important to him he felt a stunning sense of loss at the thought of never seeing her again. Nothing close to this had happened to him before, except for the way he'd felt about Jenny when they'd first been introduced.

He knew for a fact that, having met Catherine, he would pursue her under any circumstances. But with the minutes ticking away, and no sign of her, he had to conclude she couldn't bring herself to say yes to him, not even with Bonnie as the prize.

Cole unconsciously pounded the flat of his hand against the steering wheel. He could swear she was aware of the instant chemistry between them. Hell, he *knew* she could feel it. The tension between them was palpable.

But he had to remember Catherine had been deprived of her family from birth. She'd obviously struggled through her teens. Clearly she'd been let down by the man who'd impregnated her.

After the miscarriage she would have been devastated, yet she'd gone on to make a total success of her life. She couldn't have achieved her goals without using her native intelligence to make unimpulsive decisions.

By proposing marriage, he'd asked something of her that meant she not only had to let go of old fears, she had to trust him and herself enough to face the unknown. Hopefully the possibility of raising Bonnie was reason enough for her to make that leap of faith.

Going on the hunch that she needed more time to make up her mind, he started the car and drove three blocks to a convenience mart he'd passed on the way.

Alighting from the seat, he went inside for a cup of coffee. Once back behind the wheel, he decided it was time to make the phone call he'd been putting off. Whether she was at work or home, he could reach her on her cell.

She picked up on the second ring and said hello.

"Brenda? It's Cole."

"At last— I know how much you're hurting. I guess I was beginning to wonder if I'd hear from you before the weekend."

This was the last time.

"Buck's death has set me back, no doubt about it. But I'm dealing with another issue right now." He paused. "I'm afraid it's going to prevent me from seeing you again."

"You don't need to lie to me," she said in a brittle tone. "I know I don't measure up to Jenny. No woman does."

Her comment didn't faze him. Like a glorious rainbow over the Rubies following the most violent of storms, Catherine's unexpected appearance had changed the entire landscape of his life.

But Brenda didn't need to know that. He expelled a controlled sigh. "I'm sorry."

"So am I. It's been ten years. You should have gotten over her by now, Cole."

The sound of the click came as a relief.

He finished his coffee, then backed away from the curb and headed for Catherine's once more.

Bringing another colleague up to speed on the case coming into Girls' Haven had taken longer than Catherine had realized. It was six-twenty before she turned the corner of her street so fast her rear wheels squealed.

She strained to discover if Cole's rental car was parked out in front. When she couldn't see it, her heart pounded sickeningly. He'd said six o'clock and it appeared he'd meant it!

Suddenly any misgivings she might still have been entertaining about the wisdom of marrying him vanished. She wanted Bonnie, and so help her she wanted Cole too, but it looked like she was too late!

He would have come for an answer. Not finding her here, he'd gone. For all she knew he was halfway to the airport and she'd never see him again—

Like a drowning victim her life flashed before her, giving her glimpses of the three of them living in that glorious piece of heaven. But the thrill of it only lasted a moment, because it was a dream she hadn't reached for in time.

Too many old demons about trust issues had clouded her thinking. She'd taken too long to make up her mind. Now all could be lost.

Shattered by the realization, she doubled over the steering wheel in pain. She might not have known Cole for more than a few days, but she knew enough to understand he was a man of action.

Once he made up his mind about something, he didn't deviate from it. Those who couldn't meet that high standard were left in the dust. One way or another he would claim his brother's child, only Catherine wouldn't be a part of it, and it was her fault.

Maybe it wasn't too late to catch up to him, wherever he was—

Unfortunately he'd never given her his cell number. If she

wanted to get in touch with him she would have to phone the ranch and leave a message.

But she didn't dare do that. Cole had done everything to ensure this matter remained ultra-private. Too much was at risk for her to make a call that might alert his family and raise unwanted questions.

Barring another visit to the ranch, which would be a disaster, she didn't know how to contact him without letting anyone else know.

Unable to stem the tears gushing down her hot cheeks, she opened the car door with every intention of making it inside her condo before someone saw her. But as she swung her legs out into the heat, she found her way blocked by a powerful male body.

"Cole—" she cried, on a little sob of joy he couldn't have helped but hear.

He stared down at her, studying her moist face with an intensity she could feel travel the whole length of her body.

"How am I supposed to interpret those tears?" he asked in a thick-toned voice.

The time for truth had come. She would never get another chance.

"I was late b-because I had a lot of thinking to do."

Like the sun penetrating a dark cloud, his eyes filled with light. "But the point is, you came."

She moistened her lips nervously. "I had to. I love Bonnie too much to let her go without a fight. If I become your wife, we'll have the optimum chance to win custody."

Beneath the expensive brown silk sport shirt he was wearing, his chest rose and fell visibly, a sign of vulnerability she wouldn't have guessed at considering he kept such a tight control on his emotions.

"We'll be taking solemn vows in a little while. There'll be no going back," he declared with a refined savagery, reminding her he was a cattle king with an iron hand and those exceptional gifts. The idea that he was about to become her husband sent another shiver through her body.

"No."

"If the judge grants our petition, our marriage is for real." His eyes trapped hers. "You do understand that?"

She knew what he was asking. Her breath got trapped in her lungs. "Yes."

He straightened away from the door. "Good. Let's get you inside so you can pack."

"Pack?"

"After the ceremony we'll be staying at the Atlantis Reno to enjoy our honeymoon. Only you and I will know what goes on behind closed doors at the hotel. Hopefully Bonnie will be ours in a matter of days."

She froze. "I thought the whole point was to do all this in secret. If we check in there, you're bound to be recognized."

One corner of his mouth curved, almost knocking the breath out of her. "It could happen. More to the point, you and I have to make this look as romantic as possible. That's why I booked a luxury suite in the Concierge Tower there. It will help carry off the myth that we've been secret lovers over the past twelve months. Our family and friends will expect that we celebrated our marriage in the open like any besotted newlyweds."

Her legs almost buckled. "Since you live so far away from Reno, is anyone going to believe we ever had a relationship?"

"I've been flying here on personal business to see my uncle three to four times a month for years," he confided. "Finally the family will understand why I was willing to console myself away from the ranch as often as I did. My brother John and his wife Rosemary will be delighted with our news."

Not so the women who would like to be Cole's exclusive love interest, Catherine surmised.

"Bonnie's going to come as a huge surprise."

His eyes softened. "She's going to breathe new life into the Farraday clan at a very critical period. So will you," he added silkily. "As for my sister Penny and her husband Rich, they'll be overjoyed I've found love again after all this time. She'll tell you she's been worried I'd end up wifeless and childless."

"Is she one of those sisters who never leaves you alone?"

A chuckle escaped, giving her the answer. Its deep male timbre excited her.

"You're lucky."

He stared down at her through narrowed eyes. "Right now I know I am." When he said things like that her insides melted.

"Maybe it's bad luck to get too far ahead of ourselves."

"I don't believe in bad luck, just bad timing."

Her thoughts reeled. If there was one man who could impress a judge and make things happen with lightning speed, it was Cole.

No sooner had he helped her from the car than Amy drove in the next parking stall. She didn't waste any time walking over to them with a flirtatious smile centered on Cole. There wasn't a woman alive who wouldn't be attracted to him.

"We meet again." Her eyes swerved to Catherine's "Aren't you going to introduce me?"

"I'm her fiancé," Cole declared, effectively negating any reason for Catherine to speak. "We're about to be married, so forgive us if we have to rush off…"

Her heart thudded at the possessiveness in his tone.

After he'd ushered her inside the condo, Catherine turned to him. "She didn't like me before. I'm afraid that encounter just made things worse."

"Since you won't be living here from now on, it's no longer your concern. You'll need to give notice at your work."

He moved too fast for her.

"I asked for a week's emergency leave for personal reasons, and got it, but until we know whether Bonnie is ours, I'll wait to call the chairman of the board who actually hired me."

"The adoption's going to happen," he stated, as if it were a *fait accompli*. His innate confidence was a sheer revelation to her. "Now, what can I do to help? Since we can drop by here any time during the week, just bring what you need for the next few days."

She paused in the doorway to the hall. "Are we getting married in one of those wedding chapels?"

"No." A simple word, but she sensed his distaste at the mere idea. He regarded her steadily. "The ceremony will take place at the judge's home, with only his wife and my attorney present."

Thank you for that, Cole.

"I'm glad," she confessed in relief.

"Once we know Bonnie's ours, we'll repeat our vows at church in Elko."

She bowed her head. "I'd like that." Suddenly his presence in her small living room was too overpowering for her to function with any coherence. "I-if you'd like to sit down and read a magazine, I won't be long," she called over her shoulder before disappearing into the bedroom.

Catherine had been making a mental list: a dress to be married in, a business suit to wear in front of his attorney, a couple of tops and pants, a nightgown and robe.

The choices staring at her from her closet were hardly awe-inspiring. The more she examined her wardrobe, the more anxious she became.

On impulse she rushed back to the living room, where she surprised Cole in the middle of the room talking on his cellphone. His glance darted to hers. "What's wrong?"

"I don't have anything appropriate to get married in."

"Then we'll buy you something in one of the boutiques at the hotel and change in our suite before we drive to the judge's residence."

"I was hoping you'd say we had enough time. I'll hurry."

Though this was more of a business merger between rational adults than the romantic elopement of two young lovers, she didn't want to embarrass Cole. He was a well-known figure. Becoming his wife would bring her into the spotlight.

There hadn't been time for them to talk about their public

life together as man and wife, but she knew enough about him
to realize he expected her to be a woman he could introduce
with pride.

She couldn't bear the idea of his friends and family thinking
he'd made a serious mistake in his choice of bride. Perish the
thought they'd feel sorry for him. For tonight she determined
to go all-out to look beautiful for him.

Earlier Cole had asked her if she understood this was to be
a "real" marriage and she'd said yes. On the outside chance it
would have to be annulled, she hadn't allowed her thoughts to
drift that far.

That was then. This was now.

She was really getting married in a little while, and found
to her shock that she wanted it to last—even if they couldn't
adopt Bonnie.

CHAPTER SEVEN

THE suite on the twenty-third floor of the hotel had adjoining rooms leading off a private lounge, both of which overlooked the Sierra Nevadas. Cole had just emerged from his room wearing a new stone-gray suit with a deeper hued shirt and silver monogrammed tie.

On the eve of his first marriage, he hadn't known the meaning of the word nervous.

This was different. He wanted Catherine to trust him. Otherwise the plan he'd devised would never come to fruition.

Up to now he was used to making unilateral decisions without looking back when certain situations demanded it. But he realized he couldn't do that with her. She'd come too far, fought too hard for her independence to imagine she'd follow blindly where he led.

He'd made a big mistake telling her she'd have to give her boss notice. She'd tossed it right back in his face.

When she'd found the fantastic soft cream crêpe dress and shoes she'd liked, and had reached for her credit card, they'd clashed because he'd told her he'd pay for them. Up had come her softly rounded chin in a mutinous gesture she probably hadn't been aware of. But he'd noticed it, like he noticed everything about her, and backed down.

Small things could grow into big ones. He would have to learn to choose his battles more carefully. They were going to be parents, with their own ideas of how things should work. Theirs needed to be a partnership of equals. If she felt he didn't respect her opinions, she'd keep her emotional distance. He refused to let that happen.

They weren't even married yet, and already he knew he wanted her in all the old ways he'd thought had disappeared when he'd buried Jenny. He couldn't wait to explore what was coming.

Whatever else you do, Farraday, just don't blow it.

He heard a sound and turned in its direction. Catherine had left her room and was walking toward him. Her eyes looked like two dazzling sapphires.

"What do you think?" She smiled. "Too much? Too little?"

He cleared his throat. "You look like a bride. But I think you don't need me to tell you your taste is impeccable."

"Thank you, Cole. You make a very striking groom. I'm going to be the envy of every female when we leave this room."

There was nothing coy or artificial about Catherine. She didn't have theatrics in her. If he took this moment to reveal the depth of his intimate thoughts where she was concerned, she'd run a thousand miles.

He'd seen her wear her silvery blond hair several ways. Tonight she'd caught it back in a loose chignon. A few strands tipped by the sun had escaped and framed her oval face, bringing out the mold of her high cheekbones.

The simple elegance of the knee-length dress with its draped neck and long flowing sleeves brought out the singing curves of her sylph-like figure.

He'd given her a corsage of creamy roses whose petals blended with her flawless complexion. She'd already fastened it to her shoulder without his help. Another signal to let him know she needed her space.

After reaching for the digital camera he'd purchased that

afternoon, he crossed the room to the glass elevator of their suite.

"It's time, Catherine."

As she moved toward him on those long elegant legs, he snapped half a dozen pictures. He planned to have one framed for his den at the house. The rest would go in an album Bonnie would come to treasure.

"Your turn," she said, taking the camera from him. "I wish I'd had this while you were playing with Bonnie." She took several shots of him.

His lips twitched. "We'll have a lifetime to immortalize ourselves."

A worried expression crossed over her face as she handed the camera back to him. "I hope so."

"Believe it." He grasped her hand to draw her in the elevator, aware of a latent fire building inside him.

"After the ceremony we'll bring my attorney back here to do the paperwork. That way he can file it with the court first thing in the morning and get a date for a hearing with the judge right away."

"Congratulations, Mr. and Mrs. Farraday. May your life together be one of joy and happiness."

The judge who had married them spoke with an eloquence that had added the right amount of reverence and dignity to their wedding ceremony. Both he and his wife were very gracious and conveyed a sincere cordiality.

Catherine muttered her thank-you, but after the thorough kiss Cole had just given her, her palms ached and her legs had grown weak.

She'd known how important it was they give a convincing performance of being in love. It was shocking how easily she'd entered into her part of it, and she only had herself to blame if she was still trembling.

Cole's attorney Jim Darger, an attractive man in his fifties, who knew their secret and was totally loyal to Cole, had taken several pictures of them. She feared he might have caught that kiss which had lasted far too long for two people who hadn't been in each other's arms yet, let alone shared intimacy.

The moment she'd felt Cole's sensual mouth coaxing hers apart, a quickening in her body had driven her to respond without conscious thought. The urge to meld with him wasn't something she'd had control over. It had simply happened.

She must have shocked him, because he'd clasped her tighter against his rock-hard physique—whether to hold himself up or her, she wasn't sure. All she knew was that the full contact of arms, legs and mouths had charged every atom, whipping up a storm of desire in her she'd never experienced in her life.

The sound of someone's cellphone ringing had insinuated itself into the very private party Catherine had been having with her new husband. The reminder that they weren't alone had caused her to pull away from him, her face instantly burning.

Three people had just witnessed something Catherine couldn't explain. You didn't kiss a man like you were starving for him unless—unless the physical attraction was explosive. Even then she should have been able to slow down her response.

Once goodnights were said, Cole's arm hugged her waist as they walked out to the limo with Jim. During the ride back to the hotel the two men talked ranch business while Catherine studied the new diamond ring circling her finger.

He'd given her a two carat solitaire, a stone whose facets caught the light. It was exquisite. The slim gold band next to it reminded her she had some shopping to do. Before tomorrow evening she intended to present him with his own wedding ring. Maybe one with a garnet.

From what she'd learned, the Ruby Mountains were named for the red garnets found by some of the early explorers. A ring would let all those women know he was taken.

She groaned when she realized how possessive she'd become already. The possibility that their marriage could be annulled in the near future was anathema to her.

Before long they arrived back at the hotel. Within the hour they'd eaten a delicious Italian meal sent up from one of the restaurants. After a waiter had cleared everything away, Jim handed them the forms to fill out. There were so many questions to answer. The background questions took forever.

"What are our chances?" she asked him anxiously.

"You have a strong case, Catherine. Cole is well known in this state, and can provide for all of you. He's the biological father's brother. You have the biological mother's notarized letter designating you as the person she wants to raise Bonnie. Your time spent in the ICU where you bonded with the baby will stack the deck a little more in your favor. Bonding is the crucial issue in adoption cases."

She took a shaky breath. "What might be the obstacles?"

"There aren't any," Cole insisted, his expression implacable.

"I'm afraid there is *one*," Jim asserted. The furrow between Cole's brows deepened. "It's a little like insider trading on the stock market. You know something no one else knows and make a move, leaving everyone else in the dust."

Her mouth felt unpleasantly dry. "That's what I was afraid of."

Cole jumped to his feet. "It's not a good analogy. This isn't money we're bilking out of people."

"True, but you're depriving other couples of being given a chance to be considered."

Catherine lifted beseeching eyes to Jim. "Then we've got to pray the judge will overlook that aspect when he considers the positives. I didn't force Terrie to write that letter. In fact I didn't seriously consider the idea of adopting Bonnie until Terrie was dying."

"I'll put that in the deposition and file it with these papers. Have you answered all the questions?"

"Yes."

Cole nodded.

"Then all I need are your signatures at the bottom. I'll date them."

Once she'd affixed hers she glanced at him again. "How long do you think it will take before we can get a hearing?"

He gazed at her speculatively. "Judge Lander has a busy court docket, but I think I can safely say a week."

A week…

Sensing her disappointment, Cole's hand covered hers. "Jim will get it done sooner than that."

The other man pushed himself away from the table and stood up. Smiling down at Catherine, he said, "The Farraday name will have more pull than anything I say, but I'll try my best."

"Thank you, Jim. We love Bonnie. You have no idea how much this means to us."

"I think I do." He regarded both of them fondly. "For what it's worth I applaud you for the unselfish step you're taking for that little baby. The minute I know something I'll be in touch."

"If the judge rules in our favor, the case will be sealed?"

"Absolutely. No one will have access to the record so your secret will be safe. I've known Buck for years. I attended his wedding to Lucy and understand why Cole wants his reputation protected. Now Lucy can never be hurt. It will be up to you if you ever decide to tell Bonnie her true parentage."

Catherine's gaze swerved to Cole's. He always seemed to know what she was thinking because he said, "If the time comes we feel it necessary, then we'll tell her." She gave him an assenting nod.

"Well, my work seems to be done here. I'll be going and leave you two newlyweds alone."

She got up from the table and gave Jim a hug, which he reciprocated.

While Cole walked him to the elevator, Catherine hurried into her bedroom to change. The word "newlyweds" had caused a strange flutter in her chest.

She unpinned her corsage.

After the mistake she'd made kissing Cole the way you would as a prelude to making love, the worst thing she could do was waltz out there in a minute to talk to him wearing a nightgown.

The fear that her heated response might have surprised him in a negative way gnawed at her, but she honestly hadn't been able to hold back. Embarrassed just thinking about it, she quickly removed her wedding finery and slipped on jeans, which she co-ordinated with a short-sleeved cotton sweater in a lilac color.

"What have you got there?" he asked as she darted from the bedroom and hurried over to the fridge behind the bar.

"The flowers you gave me. They're so beautiful I want them to stay fresh." She moistened a paper napkin to lay over them, then put the corsage on one of the shelves. Once the door was shut she turned to him, hoping she appeared composed. What a fraud she was.

His suit jacket hung over one of the chairs. He'd loosened the collar of his shirt and pulled the tie away. She felt his shuttered gaze from across the expanse.

"I haven't taken time off to play in a long, long time," he began. "Have you?" The question caught her off guard.

"Not that I remember."

A faint smile tugged at his lips. "That's what I thought. How would you like to fly down to Laguna Beach tomorrow? We'll spend a few days sunning in the surf. Forget our worries. It will give us some time to relax and get to know each other without deadlines."

"I'd like that a lot, but—"

"You don't want to leave Bonnie." He could read her mind.

"That sounds pathetic, doesn't it?"

"No. You're making sounds like a mother."

She rubbed her palms against womanly hips. "It's just that Bonnie has needed so much love and attention. Now that she's in foster care, I go by to see her every day, either before or after work."

His indulgent eyes had been following her movements. "Then let me suggest something closer to home. After we visit her in the morning, we could drive over to Lake Tahoe for the day and have dinner somewhere before returning to the hotel. Each day we'll go someplace different, and the day after that, until we have news. What do you say?"

She felt her heart expand. "I think you already know. It's a wonderful idea. I—I haven't known you long, but I believe you're a wonderful man." The words had come out of her mouth before she could stop them, but in all honesty he deserved to hear the truth.

"If it turns out we can adopt Bonnie, she's going to be the luckiest little girl in the world to have you for a father." She dragged her eyes away from him. "Goodnight, Cole."

Four days later they got the call from Jim to meet him in the judge's chambers for the verdict. He stood inside waiting.

Catherine's heart was beating so hard she thought she would faint. Cole put a supportive arm around her while they waited for the judge to enter.

"Be seated," he told them.

The judge took his place and put on his glasses. "Mr. and Mrs. Farraday? I've read over your adoption petition. It's an unusual case. Your recent marriage concerns me, in that the two of you haven't lived together, therefore no climate has been established to measure. On the other hand, for you to enter into this union tells me of your unqualified love for this child who has no mother or father living. I find it commendable that Mr. Farraday, an upstanding member of the community and this state, wants to father his deceased brother's child. I'm also impressed by Mrs. Farraday's impeccable record as a social worker.

"I'm further moved by Terrie Cloward's testimony that if Mrs. Farraday hadn't intervened on her behalf from the beginning of her stay at Girls' Haven she would have run away, putting herself and the baby in jeopardy. Her plea that Mrs. Farraday become the adoptive mother has been duly noted.

"I would like to say I was particularly touched by the part in Mrs. Farraday's deposition concerning her feelings for the baby while she was in the hospital those five weeks, fighting for her life. The depositions taken from the hospital staff and the temporary foster mother, Carol Wilson, not only verify her constant devotion, they assert that the baby has bonded with Mrs. Farraday. I'm of the opinion that if it's at all possible, that bond should not be broken."

He took off his glasses and leaned forward. "After weighing everything carefully, I hereby grant full custody of Bonnie Cloward to the Farradays. Let it be noted in the record that, as of today, she will bear the legal name Bonnie Farraday. Congratulations."

"Cole—"

His hand squeezed hers until she felt the new wedding band she'd bought him pressing into her skin. He had a strength he wasn't aware of, but she was so happy she didn't care.

"Thank you, Your Honor," they both said at the same time.

He smiled. "Mr. Darger? If you'll come forward, I'll give you the signed order allowing the Farradays to pick up their daughter at the Wilson home immediately."

Cole crushed her against his hard body. "We did it, Catherine," he murmured into her hair. "Little Bonnibelle is ours."

Catherine sobbed for joy. "If it weren't for you—"

"Bonnie needed both of us for this to happen."

A beaming Jim walked over to them, waving the order in his hand. Cole clapped him on the shoulder while still holding onto Catherine.

"That was a brilliant piece of work you did, getting those other depositions, Jim."

"I told you bonding was everything with this judge."

She kissed the other man's cheek. "We'll never be able to thank you enough."

CHAPTER EIGHT

COLE's four-seater Cessna glided to a flawless halt at Elko Regional Airport. He flashed the pilot his thanks for a problem-free flight from Reno. With precious cargo in the seats behind them, he hadn't wanted anything to go wrong.

He'd called ahead to his brother, asking him to meet him and bring the suburban. "Come alone," he'd advised him. "I'll explain when we see each other."

From the co-pilot's window he watched John get out and walk toward the plane. Since Catherine had agreed to marry him, the excitement filling Cole's veins kept intensifying in quantum leaps. In about a minute his hatless brother was going to get the surprise of his life.

While Catherine was busy unbuckling Bonnie's carrycot, Cole climbed out on the hot tarmac behind the pilot.

John spoke first. "Hey—long time no see."

So much had happened in the time he'd been away that Cole didn't know himself anymore.

"What's up?" Though John sounded his same old self, lines of grief were still etched in the bronzed face that resembled their brother's. It was the face of Cole's little girl.

"Plenty."

John stared at him quizzically. "You look…good. Different…" He tucked his thumbs into the side pockets of his jeans. "Mind telling me what's been going on? The family's starting to worry."

Cole sucked in his breath. "Everyone can relax. You're looking at a married man."

While he left his brother standing there dumbfounded, he turned to Catherine, who handed him the carrycot. Their eyes met in a private glance before he helped her to the ground with his free hand.

Those pure blue orbs reflected anxiety. His sent her a message not to worry.

"John?" He drew his new family toward his brother. "Meet my wife, Catherine, and our little girl."

His brother did a double take. Beneath his tan, his face paled from shock.

With the advantage of surprise on his side, Cole drew the baby out of her infant seat and cradled her in his arm, being careful that the receiving blanket shielded her eyes from the rays of a blazing noonday sun.

"Bonnibelle?" He kissed her pert nose. She'd enjoyed the flight and was awake and alert. "Say hello to your Uncle John, who's going to love you like crazy."

His brother looked with wonder into her adorable face. Cole knew the second John recognized the Farraday brand, because a strange sound came out of his throat followed by a low whistle.

In the next instant his brownish-black head reared. Awestruck hazel eyes flew from Cole to the blond vision standing next to him. They filled with male admiration before switching back to Cole again, his gaze saying it all.

"Congratulations, you two." John continued to stare at them. "You're a dark horse, you know that, bro?" he growled, before breaking into a yelp of joy, erasing the grief lines noticeable a minute ago.

The noise made the baby cry, but she settled down quickly after Cole put her against his shoulder and rubbed her back. Since they'd picked her up at the Wilsons' a few days ago, he'd spent day and night with her.

Between him taking cat naps on Catherine's couch, and her

in the bedroom, they'd alternated getting up with Bonnie for her feedings. Once installed at his house, however, their sleeping arrangements were going to change...

They'd already achieved a certain harmony that made him sensitive to the silent entreaty Catherine had just sent him.

He flashed his brother a glance. "Let's get Bonnie out of the heat. Then we'll answer all your questions."

In another minute John had helped them with the luggage while Cole assisted Catherine into the backseat. With a minor adjustment of the strap through the base, he put the carrycot holding Bonnie next to her. But he found it impossible to be this close to his wife without touching her.

Since the ceremony he'd been living for the next opportunity to satisfy his increasingly growing hunger for her. Cole wasn't above using his family to force her to play house with him. In time he would get her to respond to him when they were alone.

At the moment his brother provided a convenient audience for him to give her unsuspecting mouth a long, deep kiss. When he eventually tore his mouth from hers, John would have to have been blind not to see the blush that swept into her face before he started up the car.

Once out on the highway he gave Cole a furtive wink, obviously no longer wondering what his big brother had been doing away from the ranch all this time.

Cole grinned back. They'd always been close, and for the most part could read each other's thoughts without speaking.

"Okay." He relented at last, sensing his brother's impatience for an explanation. "What do you want to know first?"

John shook his head. He looked through the rearview mirror at Catherine. "You're the beautiful mystery woman Janine told us about—the one who came to the house the day of Buck's funeral."

Air locked in Cole's lungs while he waited for his wife's response.

"I was the unwitting intruder, yes. From the beginning Cole

and I had a stormy relationship because— Well, it doesn't matter now why. But when he asked me to marry him, I turned him down flat."

"That had to be a first!" John chuckled before glancing at Cole for his reaction.

Cole nodded. "Remember last fall, when you told me I was a hard man to be around sometimes?"

"*Sometimes*— I've said that to you more times than I can count, but I do recall you were particularly difficult to reach back then. I thought it had to do with the ongoing range war over grazing rights."

"That's a problem that never goes away," Cole muttered. "But the truth is, I couldn't take it when Catherine turned me down."

"I—I couldn't take it either," came a tremulous voice from the backseat. "I loved Cole. Saying no to him turned out to be the biggest mistake of my life. When I discovered I was pregnant, I knew I needed to tell him. But I didn't want the pregnancy to complicate the issue between us, so I kept him in the dark as long as I could. He kept coming to Reno to see me, and I continued to say no to him, all because of my stupid pride. Ultimately he found out I was expecting. That's when it got really bad, because I knew I'd hurt him by not telling him. In the end I realized I'd been a total fool. Unfortunately it took until last week to get up enough courage to ask him to marry me because we had a daughter who needed her daddy as much as I did."

Even if the story had been manufactured, the throb in her voice couldn't be faked. It reached down inside the core of Cole's psyche, moving him in inexplicable ways.

"Incredible. So how did you two meet?"

"At a resort on the north end of Lake Tahoe," Catherine volunteered.

She had to be thinking of the one they'd gone to earlier in the week while they'd been waiting to hear from Jim. She was doing such a superb job, Cole was happy to sit back and let it all happen.

"One of the condos in my fourplex had a fire. I had to find a place to stay for a few days. When I went outside for a swim, your brother was doing laps in the pool. We more or less collided."

"It was fate," Cole proclaimed with a satisfied smile.

Another low whistle issued from John's lips. "This is going to knock the family up one side of the Rubies and down the other."

By now they'd entered the property, and would be coming up on the lake soon.

"It will get Penny and Rosemary off my back."

"No kidding."

"While Catherine and I settle in at my house, do us a favor and break the news to everyone? We'll be over for dinner later."

His brother's head jerked toward him. "Your place isn't exactly set up for a baby."

"All we need for tonight is a crib. Tomorrow we'll figure out everything else."

"I'll bring over the one we used for Susie. It's in the storage room somewhere."

Cole thumped his brother on the shoulder. "Thanks."

"We appreciate your coming to pick us up," Catherine chimed in. "Cole's told me so much about his family. I've been looking forward to meeting all of you."

"You don't know the half of it. To be frank, our family has feared this day would never come!"

Cole made a grunting sound. "Now that it has, better make room for more Farradays. Bonnie's going to need a little brother or sister before long."

Brother or sister—

What?

Catherine broke out in a cold sweat.

A "real" marriage she understood. Cole might have been

giving her time to get used to the idea, but she realized he expected they'd be sleeping together soon. If only he knew that she could hardly breathe, waiting for it to happen.

However, another baby wasn't something they'd ever discussed. If he was looking forward to getting her pregnant, then they needed to talk as soon as possible.

After they'd circled the lake to the house, Cole climbed out of the suburban with Bonnie, visibly excited they were home. She could tell because that air of restlessness about him while they'd been in Reno had left him.

While John took their things inside, Catherine hung back on the porch, ostensibly to look at the view. When he reappeared he told her he'd be back with the crib.

She put a hand on his arm to detain him. "That's very kind of you, John, but I've been thinking about it, and I'd rather your family didn't know anything about us until we come over for dinner. We'll get the crib then."

Or *not*.

She trembled. It all depended on Cole's reaction once they'd talked.

His eyes danced. "You're asking me to hold back that kind of news?"

Catherine liked John a lot. No doubt she would have felt the same way about Buck.

Her eyes implored him. "Do you mind?"

"Nope. We *are* a pretty terrifying lot." Then he grinned. "Now that Cole's a married man, he might as well realize upfront he's no longer the big boss around here."

She kissed John's cheek. "Bless you."

After waving him off, she walked inside the house. There was Cole at the living room window, chatting with Bonnie while they stared out at the spectacular vista. She studied them for a minute.

He'd bonded so completely with the baby, and she to him. If there was going to be an annulment after all, the two of them would be fine.

Riddled with fresh pain, Catherine searched for the diaper bag among their suitcases. The sound brought Cole's dark head around.

"I'm pretty sure Bonnie needs changing," she explained, uncomfortably aware he could sense she was feeling guilty about something.

She spread the changing pad on the first piece of furniture she came to, which happened to be a brown leather couch. Cole crossed the expanse and laid the baby down without saying anything. Her nervousness increased so much she had trouble unfastening Bonnie's pink stretchy suit.

"H-how did I do?" she blurted.

"A propos to what?" came his deceptively mild query.

"Wh-what I told John."

"Since I wasn't out on the porch with the two of you, you must mean while we were in the car?"

She moaned. "Yes."

"I believed your account to the point I decided we'd lived your version in a parallel universe."

"If John is the litmus test, do you think we passed?" She slid a fresh diaper beneath the baby.

"What do your instincts tell you?" He answered with another question. Cole was angry. She didn't blame him. They'd had no secrets until now.

He stood by with the baby wipes and ointment, unaware of his physical impact on her senses. They were crying for the assuagement only he could give. But when he learned the truth, she might never know rapture with him.

She kissed Bonnie's tummy. "They don't. John's wonderful, just like you, but he's not my brother."

"He was snagged when you threw out the line about you asking me to marry you. John's aware it would take something that dramatic for me to get off my high horse and come crawling back to you. It was the part of your story that turned the corner for him."

Her pulse accelerated. "I'll remember that," she quipped, to cover her hectic emotions. "Won't we, sweetheart?"

When she'd finished snapping the material around the baby's tiny feet and legs, he picked her up. "Come on, Bonnibelle. It's time to give you and your mommy a tour of our home. This is where we're all going to live forever."

There was that word again.

She started to shake and couldn't stop. Cole was saying that now, but when he learned what she had to tell him...

The bachelor pad turned out to be a modern two-bedroom rambler, with two bathrooms, a den, and a great room with a wood-burning fireplace. Everything was done in a light tan color, with high ceilings and lots of bare windows giving their own close up views of the pine-tree-lined lake and the fabulous Ruby Mountains.

A sweep of open area from front room to kitchen made it seem larger. No curtains or frills. No knickknacks. Just good, basic functional living, with the beauty of the architectural design of trusswork and cutouts providing the interest.

He'd made a concession to window coverings in both bedrooms, but he'd left the blinds open. Cole was a man who worked out in the open and obviously wanted to create that same feeling indoors.

Catherine loved everything about it.

Though she could see some of her things, including her favorite McKnight painting of Corfu to add color, most of them would have to stay in storage. Of necessity having a baby in the house would guarantee a lot of clutter.

Cole had promised they'd drive to Elko to outfit the second bedroom into a nursery. For the moment it contained a twin bed and dresser, nothing more. For a niece or nephew to sleep over, perhaps?

At a glance it was clear he'd wanted no hint of past memories when he'd had this built. If he needed to touch base with his life before his wife died, all he had to do was sprint around the lake to the main ranch house.

Maybe it was wrong of Catherine, but she was fiercely glad no other woman had lived here with him.

While they finished walking around, Bonnie started making noises. "Sounds like she's hungry. You can set your watch by her."

She felt Cole's masculine chuckle resonate in every cell of her body. "Lie down in our bedroom with her. I'll bring the diaper bag." They still had several bottles of the prepared formula they'd brought on the plane. The rest was in an extra suitcase.

When they entered the room, Cole must have noticed her surreptitious glance at the king-size bed. "I bought everything new when I moved in." Meaning his wife hadn't slept in it, in case Catherine was wondering.

It was scary how fast he connected the dots, no matter how obscure to anyone else. But then he wouldn't be the head of the Bonnibelle if he didn't have that remarkable capacity necessary to run a successful cattle empire.

Meeting Catherine had kept him away from his work a long time. Yet he hadn't touched on the subject.

That was because of Bonnie. She had him wrapped so tightly around her baby finger, Catherine hardly recognized him as the forbidding security guard. One who'd been prepared to drag her from the car if she didn't confess what she was doing there the day of Buck's funeral.

Driven by pain, she now understood, and she had no doubt that man would have carried out his threat—to hell with anyone who might be watching.

But the rugged black-haired male who'd just come back in the bedroom and laid down next to her and Bonnie bore little resemblance to the other man.

After handing her the bottle, he propped his head with his hand to watch them through veiled eyes. The baby drank thirstily, making loud noises.

His mouth widened in amusement. He was such a beautiful

male. Catherine had to close her eyes against his overpowering charisma.

"You're a true Farraday, Bonnibelle. No one enjoys a good meal more than I do."

Catherine had thought he was going to say Buck, which only proved how total was the transformation from uncle to father.

CHAPTER NINE

AFTER Bonnie's feed, she was out like a light.

As Catherine's eyes slid away, they met the stormcloud gray of Cole's.

"It's time to tell me what you were doing out on the porch with John." His low, penetrating voice wasn't quite a demand. "What did I say that put you off? You were different before we even got out of the car."

She swallowed uneasily.

Cole was so intuitive she could never hide anything from him. After her experience with him the first time they met, she didn't dare hold back. He'd only find a way to get it out of her. His methods guaranteed success.

She didn't want to fight with him. Especially with the innocent baby sleeping peacefully between them.

"If you must know, you and I never talked about—about having more children."

The quiet that fell after her comment could hardly be described as comfortable. She could almost hear the air crackle with tension.

His brows arched quizzically. "Isn't that part of what a real marriage implies?"

"Yes," came the lame concession.

"So what's the problem?" he infused in an unruffled tone.

She choked out, "The problem is *me*."

"In what way?" he persisted.

"Not so loud. We're going to wake the baby."

Unable to handle the nature of their conversation being this close to him, she rolled off the bed, careful to leave Bonnie undisturbed. Cole followed her into the hall.

Before she reached the living room she felt a pair of strong male hands close over her shoulders, arresting her movements. His body heat permeated the silky material of her coffee-colored blouson. Combined with his natural scent, it all worked like an aphrodisiac on her senses.

He lifted the silvery gold strands away from her neck. "I'm the one who's been a fool," he whispered, letting his lips graze her heated skin. "I've been trying to give you time to get used to me. But it appears I've unwittingly sent the wrong signal."

"I-it's not that—" she tried to tell him, but the feel of his mouth created exquisite pleasure, robbing her of the ability to think clearly.

"Surely you know how much I want you?" His hands slid down her arms to her caress her hips. "I haven't been able to hide it. Bonnie might have been the catalyst to bring us together this fast, but believe me— I felt the desire to make love to you even as you were evading my questions in front of the ranch house."

"Cole—" she cried in absolute panic. Much as his admissions thrilled her, she couldn't let this go on.

His hands stilled against her trembling body. "What is it? I know you want me too. It isn't something you can hide."

"I—I'm not trying to. But first there's something I have to tell you that could change everything."

He twisted her around. She glimpsed silvery eyes molten with desire. "Don't be silly," he murmured against her lips, gripping her waist to bring her against him.

With undeniable mastery he explored her mouth, tasting and finding every part of it. The fire he'd lit was starting to engulf her. This was a husband's kiss, hot with desire.

Her husband. A man who might not want to claim that title once he'd heard what she had to tell him.

"Please, Cole—" She fought for air, really frightened now, because she could feel herself succumbing to the wanton needs he'd aroused.

"Don't you understand I *want* to please you?" he growled softly against her ear, sending little sparks of delight through her sensitized body.

He was too drugged by passion, too intent on making love to her, to listen. With Bonnie asleep for the next few hours, there was nothing to interfere with this ecstasy.

She shivered voluptuously, because she was drowning in a sensual haze he'd created that was sapping her power to resist him. Somehow they wound up against the wall, their mouths and bodies insatiable.

"Hey, Uncle Cole—"

A young male voice called out with excitement. At first Catherine thought she must have dreamed it.

"Mom said you were back. Where've you been?"

The voice was coming closer.

Catherine struggled to surface, but she didn't make it in time.

"Oops—" the boy exclaimed.

Incredibly it was Cole who managed to ease himself away from her. Luckily she was still pressed up against the wall, which worked as a support until she could compose herself.

Cole turned to their young intruder. She could hear his ragged breathing. "Hey, Gavin—haven't you learned to knock yet before you barge in on people?"

The dark-haired boy wearing jeans and cowboy boots couldn't be more than ten. He hunched his shoulders, eyeing his uncle warily. "Sorry. I didn't know anyone else was here."

Of course the news that Cole was back had spread. But relief swept through Catherine that John had kept his promise.

"Exactly my point," Cole barked at his nephew.

Before another word was said, Catherine needed to talk to Cole in private.

"Hi, Gavin," she spoke up. "If you'll give me a minute with

your uncle, then he's all yours. Wh-why don't you go out in the living room?"

He stared at her like she was the great mystery of the ages. "Sure."

She reached for Cole's hand and drew him into the second bedroom, shutting the door behind them. When he turned to her, she hardly recognized him for his wintry expression.

His brows had formed a black bar above his eyes. "What's going on with you?" He grasped her upper arms.

Her throat tightened. "I was trying to tell you b-before you started kissing me. I didn't know having more children was included in our agreement."

She felt his fingers tighten around her flesh. "When I explained that I wanted a real marriage, you said you understood."

"I did, because I realized you meant we'd be sleeping together. But until you mentioned bringing more brothers and sisters into the world I had no idea you'd included that as part of it."

For a second she thought she saw a glint of pain in those cloudy depths.

"I guess I should have known, but all I had on my mind at the time was Bonnie." She tried to swallow but couldn't. "Naturally it's your dream to rear a family. So what I'm trying to tell you is that it's still not too late to annul our marriage. That's why I asked John not to say anything to the family yet."

Cole's hard mouth had taken on a whitish tinge. He was livid. She didn't blame him.

"I'm going to leave for Reno in the next few minutes. All you have to do is explain to Gavin I'm the woman who had your baby, but we couldn't work things out. After considering what was best for Bonnie, we decided to let you raise her."

His eyes had formed slits, which caused her to speak faster and faster. "In private you can tell John the whole truth and this will all be over."

Her eyes glistened, but she refused to cry in front of him. "You've won Bonnie legally. She's where she should be. I'm glad I was the one who could help you, but you're not in love with me. In time the right woman will come along. Love will happen naturally, the way it's supposed to. She'll fill that ache in your heart and give you the family you dreamed of having with Jenny."

"What's this about?" came a voice of ice. "Your idea of revenge for the man who destroyed your dreams?"

She backed away from him, shaking her head. "You couldn't really have asked me that question. I'm doing this to help you attain *yours*. To satisfy your curiosity, the man you think I was involved with was a pathetic teenager my own age. It was the first time for both of us, and from every aspect a miserable mistake. Telling him I was pregnant scared both of us to death. I never saw him again."

Maybe she imagined a momentary bleakness lurking in the recesses of his eyes.

Taking advantage of his bemused state, she rushed past him and opened the door. Before he could stop her she made it down the hall to the living room.

Gavin was sitting on one of the chairs, playing with a small, battery-operated video game. He flashed her a surprised glance. She smiled at him, reached for her purse and suitcase and flew out the front door. By the time she made it to the truck, Cole was almost at her heels.

If the gods were kind, it would be unlocked.

They were more than kind. His keys were in the ignition.

"Whoa, Uncle Cole. Was she ever mad!"

"She's scared."

Catherine reminded him of a graceful filly who needed special handling to get her to come to him willingly. It was his own fault for pushing every damn button guaranteed to make her skittish.

Gavin looked up at him. "Of you?"

"Not exactly. It's complicated."

He pulled out his cellphone and called Mack.

"Hey, boss—glad you're back."

"It's good to be home, but I'm without transportation at the moment. Do me a favor and catch up to the woman driving my power wagon. If you hurry you'll reach her before she hits the highway."

"What woman would that be?"

"My wife."

Mack chortled. "Hey, Cole—it's me you're talking to."

"Don't I know it. I'm counting on you to manage the impossible."

After a pause, "I'm on my way. Then what am I supposed to do?"

"Bring her back to my house."

"What if she doesn't want to come?"

"She will. Tell her Bonnie woke up feverish and is inconsolable."

"Who's Bonnie?"

"Our daughter."

"Maybe I'm in the middle of my own dream."

"It's no dream. I got married in Reno. Tell you about it later." He clicked off.

Gavin was all eyes. "You really got married?"

"I sure did. Want to come and take a peek at your new little cousin?"

Catherine had the turnoff from the Bonnibelle in her sights when a truck barreling down the road behind her whizzed past, kicking up dust. She couldn't believe it when the driver started to make a U-turn in front of her, forcing her to apply the brakes.

An authentic cowboy, maybe late forties, jumped down from the cab. He strode toward her in a well-worn Stetson.

Cole had sent him, of course. She was surprised she'd gotten this far before being apprehended. No one walked out on Cole.

She dashed the moisture from her cheeks, but anyone with eyes could see she'd been sobbing.

He approached her, removing his hat. Squinting at her, he said, "Good afternoon, Mrs. Farraday."

That was all she needed to hear. The feathers were out of the pillow now. Air rushed from her lungs.

"I'm Mack Irvine, by the way."

Cole's ranch manager...

"How do you do, Mack?"

He held the hat in front of the brown plaid shirt covering his chest. "Cole says you need to get back to the house quick. Your daughter woke up and started to cry. He's pretty sure she's running a fever and needs you."

Catherine didn't believe it for a second, but she had no desire to argue with the man Cole not only revered but depended upon. What went on between her and her husband shouldn't have to upset the running of his ranch. Especially when the histrionics were a by-product of her own flawed nature.

She'd run away. Just like she'd done over and over during her teenage years. When she couldn't deal with reality, her answer was to take off. Apparently certain patterns couldn't be broken no matter how hard she'd fought to change them.

But for once in her life she had to go back and face the consequences. She owed it to Cole, who'd been nothing but wonderful to her and deserved to hear all the truth that was in her. What he decided to do with that knowledge wasn't her right to determine.

"Thank you for telling me," she said quietly. "I'll turn around."

Mack looked vastly relieved. He nodded, put on his hat and walked back to his truck.

CHAPTER TEN

COLE saw the power wagon coming from a long way off. While he waited for his wife to materialize, he made coffee, then propped his hip against the counter while he drank it.

At long last he was going to have the luxury of being in his own home with Catherine. No more interruptions, no deadlines.

Thanks to Rosemary, who'd come for Gavin and had gone crazy the second she'd laid eyes on the baby, she'd taken everyone home with her. No doubt at this moment the whole family was marveling over the latest addition to the Farraday clan.

Cole's eyes smarted. Maybe Buck was looking on too, from wherever he was.

He heard the truck pull up in front. In a moment footsteps sounded on the porch. She hadn't come charging back. He braced himself, not knowing if that was a good or bad sign. He'd married a complicated lady.

"Hi." The husky voice he'd loved from day one sounded deeper than usual.

"Hi yourself." He studied her where she was standing next to the kitchen table. She'd been crying her eyes out. He lifted a mug. "Coffee?"

"No, thank you." He could see her throat working. "Cole—"

"Bonnie's been kidnapped by the family. We'll be lucky if we see her again before sometime tomorrow. Gavin thinks she looks like his dad. Rosemary insists she's the image of Penny.

You have to wonder how long it will be before someone says she resembles Buck."

A little sob escaped her throat. "I see you in her already."

"Spoken like a loyal wife."

She flinched. "I didn't give a very good impression of one earlier. Forgive me. I didn't mean to run away like that. I'm afraid it's an old habit when I don't want to face something unpleasant."

Sucking in his breath, Cole put the mug down. "Is the idea of getting pregnant again repugnant to you?"

She subsided into the nearest chair. "No."

His frustration grew. "Are you afraid of intimacy because of your former experience?"

"I-it's not that," she stammered.

He rubbed the back of his neck where the muscles were bunched. "Then it's me. You wanted Bonnie enough to marry me, but now the reality is too much for you to handle. Is that it?"

She flashed him a tortured look before she jumped up from the chair. "I don't think I can have more children—that's why!"

Her answer flooded him with such great relief it took him a moment to respond. Unfortunately she read something else in that brief silence.

"You see?" she cried in undeniable turmoil, staring at him with wounded eyes. "I had sex with a boy, and my high-risk pregnancy probably ruined me for any more. My punishment for doing something I knew was wrong. But I didn't know how wrong until you talked about providing Bonnie with a brother or sister."

Tears gushed down her cheeks. "Do you have any idea how it killed me to hear you tell your brother you were looking forward to having a bigger family wh-when I was afraid we couldn't? And all because it was *my* fault?"

The rise of hysteria in her voice propelled Cole toward her.

He crushed her in his arms. "Have you been checked recently by an OB who's of the same opinion?"

She burrowed her head against his shoulder. "No. I've been afraid to."

He rubbed her back in an attempt to console her. "Medical science has come a long way in the last decade to make conception possible for millions of couples. You know that."

"I don't think it's far enough for us, Cole." She sobbed against him, wetting his shirtfront. "That's why we need to get an annulment. My past mistake shouldn't prevent you from having the life you want."

She threw her head back to look at him.

What he wanted was to take away the pain from her drenched blue eyes. "I've got everything I want right here in front of me. The rest we can work out. Who knows? Maybe I'm infertile."

Her hands formed fists against his chest. "Don't be ridiculous! Haven't you heard anything I've been saying? You're too good a man to have married me. I'm like a tumbleweed out on the desert. I came from somewhere, but who knows where? I've rolled along here and there, with every gust of wind. I know nothing of my roots, whereas you can point back to your Farraday ancestors with pride."

Her trembling body bespoke her agony.

"Catherine—"

"Let me finish. I sensed how honorable you were the first time we met. You're a breed apart from any man I've ever known. Bonnie will never know how blessed she was that you claimed her. But when she grows older, what will be her opinion of a mother with no family, no clue to her background?"

He clasped her face between his hands. "Listen to me—what matters is what you've made of yourself! That's all that matters where any human being is concerned! Knowing your pedigree doesn't give you a pass in this life, Catherine. We all make mistakes. I've made a ton of my own. Some I'm not particularly proud of. Until you came into my life, I was a mess."

She shook her head. Her eyes were still swimming in tears. "I don't believe it."

"Gavin could tell you. So could the other children—*Uncle Cole's mean.*"

She sniffed. "If you're so awful, how come he came running into the house whooping it up because you're back?"

"Because children are forgiving. Haven't you noticed?"

"Yes," she confessed.

"Adults have a much harder time of it. I know one woman who needs to forgive herself so she can make this man happy." He kissed her luscious mouth. "I'm in love with you, darling. So much it hurts."

"But you can't be—"

"Let's get something straight, then we never have to talk about it again. If this weren't the real thing, I wouldn't have asked you to marry me under any circumstances. After meeting you, I discovered I wanted you, long before I saw Bonnie. The second I saw her, I wanted her too. Since then I've tried to show you in every way but one. Maybe going to bed will help."

Her eyes grew slumberous. "I think it will." She slid her arms around his neck. "Oh, Cole—" She pressed kisses all over his handsome face. "I've been wanting you to make love to me forever—I adore you." Her voice shook. "You have no idea how much."

For an answer, his mouth came down on hers, urgent and avid. Flames of desire licked her veins, turning her into a breathless supplicant. She didn't remember being carried to the bedroom. All she knew was that she was in his arms, trying to satisfy her craving for him.

Hours later, when the stars had faded over the Ruby Mountains and the sun was about to come up, she had to give herself a talk about leaving him alone. He was in a deep sleep at last.

She should have been sated by now, yet she realized the craving for him was worse than before and would never go away.

Out of the semidarkness she heard a velvet voice whisper, "Come here." Cole pulled her on top of him, trapping her legs.

Her breath caught. "I didn't mean to waken you."

"That's the first lie you've told me all night," he teased, kissing her in a certain spot.

Her face crimsoned. "Do you know how embarrassing it is to want your husband so much you have no shame?"

"There's no shame when two people love each other as much as we do. Only a hot-blooded woman like you could ever hold me. When my time comes—"

"Stop—" She put a hand over his mouth. "I don't ever want to think about that."

He pressed a moist kiss to her palm. "Naturally I'm hoping it won't be until after a lifetime of loving. But when it does happens—remind me to thank my little brother. Without him I would never have known this kind of happiness."

"Cole, darling—" she cried in an aching voice.

Once again her world spun away in a ritual of giving and taking and unspeakable pleasure. Catherine's entrancement was so total she didn't realize at once that someone was ringing the doorbell.

"Sweetheart—"

"Ignore it and they'll go away. I have other things to do," he whispered, plundering her mouth.

The bell pealed again.

"Cole?" She tried to breathe. "I think we'd better get it. Maybe something's wrong with Bonnie."

"Someone would have phoned."

"Maybe it's Mack."

A groan escaped. "All right. I'll get it." He pressed another hungry kiss to her mouth before rising from the bed.

She watched her gorgeous husband shrug into a toweling robe and leave the bedroom. In another minute she could hear Cole say, "Gavin—where's the fire?"

"The family wants you and Catherine to come over for breakfast, but they were afraid you wouldn't answer the phone."

"Then why didn't you just come in and tell us?"

"But yesterday you told me not to barge in!"

"That was yesterday."

"You don't sound mad anymore. I guess she's not afraid of you anymore either?"

"Nope."

"That's good, huh?"

"Yup."

Catherine had to cover her mouth to hold in her laughter. If this was how things were going to be on the Bonnibelle from now on, she could handle a hundred lifetimes of it.

* * * * *

LUCY GORDON
Playboy's Surprise Son

Lucy Gordon cut her writing teeth on magazine journalism, interviewing many of the world's most interesting men, including Warren Beatty, Charlton Heston and Roger Moore. She also camped out with lions in Africa, and had many other unusual experiences that have often provided the background for her books. Several years ago, while staying in Venice, she met a Venetian who proposed in two days. They have been married ever since. Naturally, this has affected her writing, where romantic Italian men tend to feature strongly.

Two of her books have won the Romance Writers of America's RITA® award.

You can visit her website at www.lucy-gordon.com.

CHAPTER ONE

'THE race is nearly over. The two drivers from the Brent Team are neck and neck. Jared Marriot of Team Cannonball seemed bound to win, but he faded and his challenge is over—*no, here he is!*—catching up with the front two. Has he enough room to pass? Yes, there he goes, streaking ahead of them both, and there's the chequered flag to say that he's won.'

Colours flashed across the television screen as the Cannonball car shot over the finishing line, closely followed by the two Brent cars. The camera honed in on Jared Marriot, waving a hand above his head, fist clenched in victory.

'He did it, Mummy.' Mike, the little boy on the sofa, was beside himself with glee. 'He won! I knew he would.'

'Of course you did, darling,' Kaye assured her son.

'He always wins, doesn't he?' Mike insisted.

'Well,' she said cautiously, 'not quite always.'

Mike glared indignantly. 'Yes, he does,' he insisted. 'Always.'

Kaye smiled fondly. At five years old, Mike thought he could make the world do as he wanted. Jared Marriot was his hero, which meant that he won every race, even when he didn't.

They watched as he climbed out of the car to be greeted with wild acclaim from the team, then leapt up onto the podium and sprayed champagne everywhere—the very picture of triumph.

In the interview that followed he was engagingly modest.

Yes, he'd had a few unfortunate incidents lately, but the bad times were behind him. He'd won the World Championship three times, and as for this year—well, we'd see. He said the last words with a knowing twinkle in his eye that made everyone laugh with him, not at him.

That was his gift, Kaye thought wistfully. His laughter was an invitation to join him in a merry conspiracy, and it would take a heart of stone to refuse.

Her heart had never been made of stone, not where the young Jared had been concerned. They'd shared one evening, and the sense of being close to him had been intense and beautiful, making her want to be closer yet, and closer.

Was it really his fault that it had all been an illusion? She'd been eighteen—old enough to have some common sense, so she'd told herself in the despair that engulfed her afterwards. She refused to blame him, for if she did so she would lose something she couldn't bear to lose.

Mike was still burbling happily about his hero.

'Mum, when can I drive a racing car?'

'When you're a lot older than you are now,' she said firmly.

'And then I'll be like Jared?'

'If you're crazy enough, yes,' she teased.

She wondered at his fixation with one man. There were lots of other daredevil racing drivers. Perhaps he'd noticed that Kaye always watched Grand Prix races, eyes following Jared, and that she tensed up if he had an accident.

Or perhaps there was another reason…

Later that night, when she'd seen Mike safely asleep, Kaye returned to the television and switched on the recording she'd made of the race so that she could watch it again later, when she was safely alone. There was Jared in triumph. When the camera homed in on his face she paused the picture and watched it with an aching longing.

This was the man she remembered from nearly six years ago: a little older, affected by the terrible tragedy that had nearly

killed him last year, but still basically the wild and wacky
character who'd entranced her from the first moment.

She'd been enjoying a gap year before heading for university
to develop her talent for languages. It was that very talent that
had won her a job with Brent. Car racing took place in many
countries, and an employee who could slip easily from one
language to another was useful.

That was how she'd met Jared. He'd been in Monza for the
Italian Grand Prix, along with Brent's other driver, a great name
in the sport—known as Warrior and self-obsessed. He had a
lucky charm—a silver badge worn under his racing gear—
and when he'd accidentally left it behind there'd been a crisis,
resolved by sending Kaye to Monza.

There she had endured Warrior's effusive thanks and spent
the next day being treated as his multi-lingual servant.

Second driver on the team had been a young man with laughing eyes and film star looks.

'Jared will be a fine driver when his time comes,' Warrior
loftily declared. 'He just needs to be a little patient.'

Jared, overhearing, grinned and winked at Kaye. In the race
he came within an inch of defeating Warrior, who emerged
from his car pale and ill-tempered.

'He's not going to forgive you for that,' Kaye murmured as
they all got ready to leave the track.

Jared chuckled. 'Wait until the next race. Maybe I can give
him something else not to forgive. Bye!'

He blew her a kiss and hurried away to join the glamorous
model who was waiting for him, which gave Kaye a stab of
jealousy. Her own looks were pretty enough, but she knew she
couldn't attract a man who could take his pick from a wide
choice.

For a few weeks she watched Jared's progress through the
races, which he won—to Warrior's ill-concealed fury—and
through a few colourful explosions in the tabloids featuring
various curvaceous companions.

She sometimes met him briefly in England, between races.

He would recognise her from a distance, wave and be gone. Once he bought her a cup of tea in the firm's canteen and she enjoyed a few dazzling minutes with him, only slightly spoiled when he addressed her by the wrong name.

Clearly she just didn't have the 'something' that made a girl stand out from the crowd. If only she was more rounded.

'Much too thin,' she told her reflection in the wardrobe.

'You count your blessings,' her grandmother said, just behind her. 'There's many a plump girl would say you were lucky.'

Her mother's parents had raised her since her own parents had died in a road accident eight years before. Their relationship was affectionate, with no more than the normal inter-generational exasperation on both sides.

'You can wear those tight jeans, which is more than most of them can,' Gran observed helpfully.

'Only 'cos I'm shaped like a boy,' Kaye said in disgust. 'No ins, no outs, no nothing!'

'Good. It'll help you stay out of mischief.'

One by one Jared's victories mounted: Turkey, Italy, Belgium, Brazil. Between races the press pursued him intently, attracted by the stream of lovelies in his company. One in particular alerted them. Mirella, a model as famed for her colourful life as for her beauty, appeared on his arm more than any other. There were quarrels, reconciliations, even talk of marriage—all of it featured in the headlines. When he won the Japanese Grand Prix, inches ahead of Warrior, Mirella was there to greet him in the pits.

Returning to England, Warrior went into a sulk which ended in him storming into the office one evening as Kaye was about to leave, having worked late. She indicated that Duncan, her boss, was still there, and Warrior headed for Duncan's office, slamming the door behind him.

At once voices were raised and she listened, fascinated, to the ensuing row. It might be shocking to eavesdrop, but how often could you get entertainment this good?

At last, reluctantly, she headed for the exit, colliding with someone she hadn't noticed before.

'Sorry,' Jared said, steadying her.

'How long have you been there?'

'Just a few minutes. I was going to talk to Duncan but—' he made a face '—perhaps another time.'

'Warrior's really mad at you for overtaking him when you did,' she said softly.

'It was a race. I'm supposed to overtake.'

'But he's the number one driver, so you should have let him stay ahead.'

'In his dreams. Oh, Lord, they're coming out. Quick!'

He grabbed her hand, whisking her away before she could protest. Not that she wanted to protest. Now she was with him again she knew how she'd longed for this.

The two men emerged and headed for the elevator. Neither of them saw Jared and Kaye, keeping well back.

'You're not doing anything tonight, are you?' he asked when they were safely alone.

It was more an arrogant statement than a question. If he wanted her, how could she possibly be doing anything else? But she was too dazzled by him to see anything wrong with that.

'Not a thing,' she assured him.

'Then let's get out of here fast.'

She went with him eagerly, terrified lest anything happened to change his mind. A small bar had recently opened across the street, and they took refuge there.

'Thank heavens I didn't walk into a scene!' he said thankfully when they were settled.

'Don't tell me you're afraid.'

'Of scenes? Sure. I avoid them like the plague.'

'And they call you the bravest man on the track,' she teased.

'Ah, on the track! That's different. Crashing at two hundred miles an hour, no problem. But raised voices and agitation—' He shuddered. 'I just run for it.'

'You weren't expected for a day or two,' she said. 'We all thought you'd be kept fully occupied by—er—' She was carefully avoiding Mirella's name.

'All right, all right,' he said, understanding perfectly and grinning. 'I made a hasty exit. Can we leave it?'

She burst out laughing and his grin became more relaxed.

'I'm a coward there too,' he admitted. 'In fact I'm just a disreputable character, and I can't think why anyone bothers with me.'

'Neither can I,' she declared solemnly. 'From where I'm sitting, you have absolutely nothing going for you.'

'I know.' He sighed. 'Women turn away from me, and somehow I just have to endure it.'

He was twenty-four, with the lean figure of an athlete and looks that retained the barest hint of boyishness. His dark brown eyes seemed to contain mysterious depths, even when they gleamed with fun, as they did now. Female rejection was something he would never experience and they both knew it.

He was wry, funny, ridiculous, self-mocking, and—most charming of all—he seemed to give her all his attention. Common sense warned her that it meant nothing, was merely something he did with everyone, especially women. But she firmly silenced common sense. Who needed it?

They chatted easily. It was the talk of friends, not lovers, but she was happy. When their eyes met in amused understanding she had a sweet sensation that should have warned her of danger. But she only realised that later. Much, much later. When it was far too late.

'Driving my first racing car was like reaching heaven,' he recalled. 'I was free. I could do what I liked. Mind you, what I liked was usually stupid, and there was trouble afterwards, but it was worth it. I knew I had to drive cars for a living, one way or another.'

'You could have become a taxi driver,' she told him, straight-faced.

He struck his head. 'Hey, I never thought of that! What a chance I missed! All those crashes when I could have been doing something really interesting. Mind you, there's a snag. In a taxi the passenger is the boss. I can't stand that. I have to be in charge.'

'But don't you get instructions from the team?'

'They tell me what they want, but I contrive to do it my way. I'm the one in the driving seat and they just have to get used to that.'

Another man might have sounded like a bully. Jared merely came across as a charming lad who would manipulate his own way by one means or another.

A giggle from another part of the bar made them look up to find that he'd been recognised.

'Oh, no,' he groaned. 'Come on.'

Grabbing her again, he whisked her out onto the pavement, suddenly overcome by self-reproach.

'I've got no manners, have I? That's twice tonight I've just hauled you away without asking what you want.'

'I'm not complaining.'

'That's because you're a sweet, understanding person, but you deserve better than me.'

She suppressed the instinct to say, *No, I don't. Ever.* She was in a haze of delight.

'At least I can offer you something to eat,' he said. 'Come—' He stopped in the act of seizing her hand, groaning. 'I'm doing it again.'

'Well, you'd better get on and do it, then, hadn't you?' she said, laughing and grasping his hand in her turn. 'Where are we going?'

'To my home. No more public places.'

'Where are you parked?'

'I live nearby. No driving. Which is just as well because—' he blinked '—I may have had just a little too much wine.'

His home turned out to be a couple of rented rooms, which astonished her by their austerity.

'I'm hardly ever here,' he explained as she looked around. 'Every two weeks there's a race in a different country. Plus, I'll soon be moving to another team, which is what I really came to tell Duncan tonight.'

She was facing away from him so he didn't see the dismay at the news that he was leaving.

'Right,' he said breezily. 'It's time for me to demonstrate that I have other skills besides acting like a maniac on the track.'

To her surprise he turned out to be a skilled cook.

'My mother insisted on it,' he explained. 'She said women would find me such a turn-off that I'd better learn to fend for myself.'

Again they laughed together, and again happiness pervaded her so that nothing else mattered. Almost nothing else. The knowledge of his imminent departure lay like a threat in her mind, infusing every word and action. Perhaps it caused what happened next.

When they'd finished washing up he said, 'Bless you for everything. What would I have done without you?' Then he leaned forward and kissed her lightly.

She couldn't blame him for the consequences. They were at least as much her doing, perhaps more. Suddenly her arms were about him, her mouth pressing against his, her whole being trembling with delight and anticipation. She sensed the shock that went through him and the next moment his embrace grew more fervent, more thrilling.

They were on the sofa, undressing each other with frantic hands, reaching for the moment they were now both desperate to achieve. She gasped as they became one, but then, suddenly, it was all over. He was pulling away as though desperate to escape. She had a view of his face that she would remember all her days. It was a blank mask, except for the eyes that were full of dismay.

'We must stop this,' he gasped. 'I didn't mean to—you're all right, aren't you?'

She was far from all right. The joy had been snatched from her at the last moment and she wanted to weep, but she forced a smile.

'Yes, fine,' she lied. 'It was just—'

'I know. I didn't mean to—I didn't realise—your first time. But don't worry, I didn't—not exactly—'

Had he made love to her fully or not? In her innocence she couldn't have said, but it was plain that he wanted the answer to be no.

He couldn't get rid of her fast enough. He called a taxi and paid the fare in advance, but didn't offer to see her home. His words and manner were perfectly courteous, but it was the perfection of a mask. She wept for the whole journey.

For the next few weeks she had the sensation of seeing life at a distance: the row about Jared's departure, his last race for Brent, the Brazilian Grand Prix, which he won, making him the World Champion Driver on points.

His picture was everywhere—holding up the trophy, being embraced by Mirella, regarding her with an entranced expression. How different from his shocked eyes as he'd pulled away from herself.

She guessed that it was her inexperience that had dismayed him. It threatened involvement, emotion, scenes—things he avoided like the plague.

Even so she clung to the hope that he would contact her, even if just to say goodbye. But there was no word from him, and by the time she first suspected that she might be pregnant he'd already left without a backward glance.

A visit to his apartment was futile. Already somebody else was living there. E-mail produced only an 'address invalid' message. Clearly Cannonball had taken him over completely. In despair she made one last try, getting his mobile phone number from the firm's records and texting.

I really need to see you. It's important. Kaye

In five seconds precisely, she received a routine reply.

Thank you for contacting Jared Marriot. This number is now closed, but he thanks you for your good wishes.

On the same day his engagement to Mirella was announced, and she knew her last hope was gone. She had too much pride to force herself onto his attention. She would have his child alone. She didn't know how she was going to do it, but she'd made up her mind.

Her grandparents were magnificent, insisting that she should live with them. College had to be abandoned, but she stayed on with Brent until she gave birth.

Ethel encouraged her to return to work, but Kaye was swept by the need to be with her baby. So she left Brent and worked at home as a freelance translator. She also enrolled in the Open University, and emerged triumphantly with a degree.

Jared never married Mirella, who simply faded from the scene, to be replaced by many others in quick succession. The papers detailed every one.

Gradually Kaye learned to cope with reminders of the man who'd rejected her. She even named her son Michael, which was Jared's second name. But that was the only hint of sentimentality that she allowed herself.

At last Mike started school. When she was sure he was settled in happily she decided to return to work full-time. Only half hoping, she contacted Duncan at Brent, and he welcomed her back with open arms.

Jared was long gone from Brent, and was now only mentioned when he won yet another Grand Prix, and then another.

'Not that things are looking so good for him this year,' Duncan observed. 'He was rushed to hospital after a crash just before the season started, and nobody knows why. They say he spun off for no apparent reason. The press have gone mad trying to find out, but there's a big mystery there somewhere. Luckily it's working to our advantage, because his reactions seem a bit slower. This season he hasn't won races that he'd have won before. Now, that's enough about him. Where did I put that—?'

She got to know the other drivers, especially Hal, a pleasant man, whose wife, Stella, dropped in one day. Through their children, Stella and Kaye immediately established a bond.

It was a contented, even sometimes a happy life. In the dead of night she would creep into Mike's room to watch her darling son sleeping, and she would know that, whatever trophies came Jared's way, it was she who was the real winner.

And yet…

The air was filled with shouting, cheers and laughter. The noise surrounded Jared, battering him. But at the same time it came from outer space, taunting, threatening his sanity.

The winner's podium was his natural place. He turned this way and that, spurting champagne, stretching his mouth in a pretence of a smile, waving at the crowd, struggling to make it all feel natural, as it once had. But the echoing distance seemed to fill him with darkness.

This was his first win in four races, and should have been a triumph—the moment when he recovered everything that had been his before the nightmare. But that was impossible. He might recover much, but not everything.

He forced himself to give the performance of a hero celebrating his victory, secretly thinking, *If only they knew!*

They knew a little about the accident he'd had just before the start of the season, three months earlier. He'd been testing out Cannonball's new car when he'd swerved suddenly, overturned, and come to a shuddering halt.

Onlookers had been baffled. There were no barriers on the track, no other driver had been near him and the car was perfect. Nobody knew that Jared had been feeling ill when he started, and had soon been swamped by sickness.

At the hospital he'd been shut away from visitors. The press had speculated on the 'terrible injuries' he must have suffered, and cheered him when he'd returned quickly to racing. Nobody suspected the truth.

And nobody must ever suspect, lest he die of shame.

Outwardly he seemed to have it all: just approaching thirty, at the peak of looks ability, health. That was what people thought, and what they must go on thinking.

He headed for the airport as soon as possible. There, booked on the same flight back to England, he found Hal, the driver from the Brent Team that he'd beaten into second place.

'Sorry,' he said wryly.

'Oh, sure—if you had it to do again you'd let me win?' Hal grinned. 'I don't think so.'

He was in his thirties, with an innate good nature that stopped him being hostile to Jared, despite their rivalry. He even managed to say, 'It's good to see you back on top form after your recent troubles.'

'Thanks. They're in the past,' Jared said airily. 'I'm my old self again.'

The words *if only* echoed in his mind again before he could avoid them.

Stern resolution! Banish those thoughts! Work at it! Be strong!

'But I'm still behind in the championship,' he continued with a shrug. 'The title will probably be yours.'

'Well, it'll be nice to go out on a high,' Hal agreed.

'You're really retiring?'

'This is my last season as a driver. I'll stay with the team, working behind the scenes, but I can spend more time at home with the wife and kids.'

Jared quickly went blank inside, as he'd trained himself to do at the mention of children.

Damn the illness that had attacked him without warning. Damn every man who could become a father when he himself couldn't!

Hal had pulled out a small leather folder, flipping it open to reveal a picture of his family.

'I never go anywhere without this,' he said proudly. 'I'm not like you, chased by sexy dollybirds.'

Jared gave a fixed smile, diverting attention by taking the folder and flipping through it. Suddenly he grew still.

'Who's that?' he asked quietly.

'Who? Oh, her. That's Kaye. She used to work for Brent, left when she had a baby, and came back a few weeks ago. Stella and I got to know her because her son is the same age as our youngest and they go to the same school.'

'Her—son?'

'Yes, little Mike. Look.' He flipped over some pages. 'I took these at his birthday party recently.'

There was Kaye, a little older, but still recognisable as the eager girl he'd known way back then. She was sitting with her arms around a little boy who seemed to be consumed with laughter. She too was laughing, as though all happiness was to be found in the child.

'What about her husband?' Jared asked.

'She's not married. I don't think she ever was.' He looked back at the picture, adding, 'They had the party the day before his fifth birthday. I had to dash off for the Turkish Grand Prix next day. We were on the same plane, remember?'

'I remember.' Jared's voice gave nothing away.

Suddenly he was back in the hospital, horrified at the illness that had attacked him.

'Mumps?' he'd said, aghast. 'That's a kids' illness.'

'Adults can catch it too.' The doctor sighed. 'And you've got it badly.'

The sight of his face, swollen out of recognition, had horrified him. But worse had been the discovery of the side effects.

'In a grown man mumps can cause sterility,' the doctor warned. 'We'll do tests to be sure.'

Until the last minute he'd refused to believe that the worst could happen. But the tests showed that it had.

'Are you telling me,' Jared asked, appalled, 'that when I'm with a woman I won't be able to—?'

'Your sexual skill will be unimpaired,' the doctor said clinically. 'But that's all. Your sperm count is down to about two or three percent, maybe less, and your chance of fathering a child is virtually nil.'

Hal was flipping through the pictures again. Jared took a quick glance at the one showing Kaye and her son. The day before the flight to Turkey, Hal had said, thus revealing the date of the child's birthday.

He threw himself back in his seat, staring into space as dates came together in his head. It was surely impossible. Yet the facts danced, shrieking, before him.

The little boy had been born almost exactly nine months after his evening with Kaye.

CHAPTER TWO

HIS dreams were haunted by a face: swollen, stupid, disturbing. Strange sounds came from the mouth. Despair as everything was snatched away, fear at the helplessness, horror as the world crashed around him. The eyes were wide, the mouth crying out with despair.

Himself!

He awoke to find himself sitting up in the darkness, shuddering.

The face was his own. No! *Had been* his own, he corrected quickly. Not any more. That disgusting, off-putting fool, defenceless in the power of others, had been him for the few brief days while the illness was as its worst, but that was over. His face had returned to normal, but the memory haunted him.

Hurriedly he switched on the light and seized a mirror. Yes, that was Jared Marriot looking back at him, handsome, astute, victorious. Above all, in control. The other was a ghost that he would banish, however long it took.

Growling, he leapt out of bed and headed for the bathroom to get under the shower. He was in fine shape, lean and strong, with a body that women openly desired and other men envied.

But their envy would turn to derision if they knew that he couldn't do the one thing nature most demanded of a true man: produce the next generation.

Until now his free, self-indulgent life had been enough, and he'd given no thought to becoming a father. But the discovery that he was incapable had changed everything.

Not to care about fathering a child was one thing. Not to be able to was a humiliation.

'Will anyone be able to tell?' he'd demanded of the doctor.

By 'anyone' he meant women.

'Not at all,' the doctor said, understanding him. 'Everything will be normal, except that you're sterile.'

He'd put that to the test as soon as his strength returned. There was no shortage of willing ladies, and to his relief his performance was as excellent as it had always been. Nobody knew. Except himself.

The discovery of Mike had been like a light shining in the darkness. If that was his son, as seemed likely, he had a defence against the world's derision. And he would secure that defence come what may.

Now his mind was working as it did on the racetrack: cool, calm, efficient. Calculate everything to the tiniest degree, allow no distractions, think only of victory. *Nothing else.*

So the first thing he must do—That was it! Take the first step and the rest would be straightforward.

He stared into the bathroom mirror and Jared Marriot stared back: cool, decided, uncompromising. Unfeeling.

Except for fear.

It was the last day of Mike's school term, and he was taking part in the pageant. Kaye left work early, determined not to miss a moment. In the car park she paused and smiled up at the sun.

Then she dropped the key, astounded by what she'd glimpsed.

Stooping for it, she told herself to be sensible. Of course Jared wasn't there. She'd imagined it. And when she rose and looked round there was no sign of him.

I'm going crazy, she told herself. Seeing things.

The pageant took the form of a procession through the grounds of the nursery school. Little Mike, dressed as a cowboy, bowed and waved to the crowd of cheering parents, accepting the spotlight as his by right. Kaye reckoned that Jared's son simply couldn't help it.

That was why she'd thought of Jared today, she told herself firmly. There was no need to get hysterical.

But when she collected Mike afterwards he beamed and cried, 'Mummy, he's here.'

'Who's here, darling?'

'Jared Marriot.'

Her heart seemed to miss a beat. Were they both floating in fantasy land?

'There he is,' Mike said urgently.

She followed his pointing finger, frantically trying to decide how to deal with this. Then she grew still.

Jared was standing only a few feet away, watching her.

He was really here.

No, he couldn't be.

But he was. How was this happening?

'Ah, there you are.'

It was Stella, Hal's wife and her friend, whose son Joey attended this same school.

'I looked for you before but we were a bit late arriving,' Stella said. 'Hal brought a friend—one of the other drivers. Jared, come and meet Kaye.'

As he approached it seemed to her that he moved slowly, coming from a great distance, a ghost who haunted her and then arrived without warning. She waited for the recognition in his face, perhaps even dismay, but there was nothing. As he uttered a courteous greeting there was only unrevealing charm.

She managed to seem equally unaware, shaking his hand, trying not to be too conscious that she was touching him again after so long.

Mike tugged at Jared's sleeve. 'I'm Mike,' he said.

Jared's smile was friendly. 'I'm Jared.'

They shook hands, Jared showing as much courtesy as he would have done to an adult. Mike was in seventh heaven.

'Mike is my son,' Kaye said.

No reaction. Just a conventional smile and a nod. Clearly the discovery of her child rang no bells in his memory.

'Ah, there you are,' came Hal's voice as he bustled towards them with Joey in tow. 'They've set up a little buffet over there. Let's go.'

Mike and Joey moved with their eyes fixed upwards on Jared, stumbling a little, so that he reached out and grasped their shoulders good-naturedly.

'It's safer this way,' he said.

He guided them to a bench and sat chatting while the others went to secure soft drinks. Kaye's mind was in a whirl.

Why had he suddenly turned up now? Had she really seen him before or was that just an incredible coincidence?

'Jared and Hal get on well, even though they're on different teams,' Stella explained. 'I think he's lonely because he's got no family of his own.'

But he has, Kaye thought sadly. He has a son that he doesn't know about because he doesn't want to. He doesn't even remember me, and perhaps that is because he doesn't want to.

But a surprise was waiting for her. As they returned to the bench she handed Jared a glass of sparkling water, which he raised to her in salute.

'We've met before, haven't we?' he said.

Yes, she thought furiously. We've met before, and you went all out to charm me, then left me stranded with a child as you danced away to the next woman. Oh, yes, we've met before.

But she only said coolly. 'I didn't think you'd recognised me.'

'You worked for Brent,' he said, making room for her to sit beside him. 'I gather you've rejoined them?'

'Yes, I left when I had Mike, but I went back recently.'

'Still translating everything?'

'Sort of. I run errands for Warrior. He's part of the management now.'

'How do you stand him?'

'Not very easily. He goes on a bit about his "great days" and we all keep a straight face and pretend we don't know you took the title from him.'

Jared gave a crack of laughter, and for a moment she was back in that other time when he'd seemed to laugh as he breathed, as though the joy of life infused everything.

He was the same man, she thought. The years had merely increased his pleasures and triumphs, making him more himself, more enviable, more confident that he was king of the world. And she knew a flash of resentment so sharp that it took her breath away. How dared he be so unchanged after what he'd done to her?

Her resentment increased when she saw that he was already forgetting her. Mike had demanded his attention, wanting to hear Jared talk about his last race, and then his next.

'Valencia's going to be good,' Jared said. 'It's a winding circuit, challenging—chances to overtake.'

Kaye had to admit that he didn't talk down to Mike, but discussed the track sensibly. In the face of her little boy's blissful happiness her annoyance faded, just a little.

Soon Hal and his family were ready to leave. Jared rose to depart with them.

'Nice to see you,' he said politely to Kaye.

He gave her a nod, ruffled Mike's hair, and was gone.

'Mum, you should have asked him to come home with us,' Mike protested.

'He arrived with his friends. He has to leave with them,' she said mechanically.

Her words seemed to echo in a void. The world, so full and vibrant a moment ago, was empty and desolate again.

'Come along, now,' she said. 'Let's go home and make sure Sam's all right.'

Her grandparents had planned to attend the pageant, but Sam's sudden toothache had sent them hurrying to the dentist in alarm. But all was well. Kaye could see that as soon as she reached home.

'So it wasn't too bad?' Kaye said.

'Bad?' Ethel echoed scathingly. 'He's had the time of his life: couldn't take his eyes off that pretty nurse.'

'A man needs his pleasures,' Sam declared, getting carefully out of his wife's way.

Kaye especially loved them when they were like this: cracking jokes, chuckling together. It was typical of them that they had always wanted her to call them Sam and Ethel.

'No need to make us old before our time,' Sam had said. Which Kaye thought showed some style, considering they were in their seventies.

'There's more to love than romance,' Ethel had told her once. 'A good laugh matters just as much—well, almost.' And, watching them, Kaye knew it was true.

Over tea Mike told them all about his wonderful afternoon. They were suitably impressed. Not until the child had gone to bed did Sam say carefully, 'That is him, isn't it? Mike's father?'

The subject was never discussed. They knew, but were discreet.

'Yes, it's him.'

'Did he—you know—say anything?'

'What would he say? I've never been able to tell him, and I don't think he remembers much.' Her tone was cool and ironic.

'Perhaps it's time he knew?' Ethel suggested.

'Force it on him? No, thank you. The night it happened he wasn't completely sober, and he didn't really think we went all the way. I wasn't even sure myself until I found I was pregnant. Can you imagine trying to convince him, begging him to believe me, joining the other hopeless females who go chasing after him?'

Try as she might to speak rationally, the note of bitterness crept into her voice.

'You really hate him, don't you?' Sam said gently.

'No, I don't hate him. I'm just angry. Who does he think

he is, walking back after years away? Acting like he's some sort of deity and we're all supposed to gasp and applaud. I've managed very well without him so far, and I'll manage even better in future.'

'Aren't you being a bit hard on Jared?' Sam asked.

'Hah! If only you could have seen him. He barely remembered me. Oh, he put on a good performance, but I could tell he was scrabbling around in his memory. I won't hear from him again and that suits me fine.'

'Well—time for bed,' Ethel said.

Kaye bade them goodnight, took a final look at the sleeping Mike, then went downstairs to sit in the garden, gazing up at the moon, wishing with all her heart that she hadn't met Jared again. His second rejection would be a thousand times harder to take.

Her cell phone rang.

'It's me,' he said. 'I'm just across the road.'

Answers jangled in her head. *Who do you think you are? Go away, I'm finished with you. You've got a nerve.*

'I'm just coming,' she whispered.

The house faced a park. Emerging from the front door, she could see him standing beneath the trees, watching for her. The light of the full moon was just enough to show that he was full of tension, which seemed to ease as she came nearer. At last she saw him smile, and wondered if he was really overwhelmed with relief—or was that just his usual charming act?

Be careful, warned her inner voice. Don't trust him for a moment.

'I thought you'd be long gone,' she said, trying to sound indifferent.

He made a face. 'Here today and gone tomorrow, that's me. Most of the time anyway. But sometimes it's nice to linger and talk about old times. It's good to see you again. Look what I brought you.'

He held up a bottle of wine, the very same kind they had drunk that other night.

'You said this was your favourite,' he reminded her.

'How did you ever remember that?' she gasped, touched even against her will.

He grinned. 'I guess I just—remembered.'

No man had the right to be so charming. It wasn't fair. But she was on her guard.

'There's a bench over there by the pond,' he said. 'Let's sit down. Give me your hand.'

She did so, but reluctantly. Touching him was dangerous.

By moonlight they made their way to the bench and he poured the wine.

'Sorry they're only plastic cups,' he said.

'Mmm. Delicious.'

'Let me look at you,' he said, twisting on the bench and turning her gently with his hands on her shoulders, so that they were facing each other. Leaving his hands there, he studied her, his head on one side, then on the other, smiling, as if to tell her not to be offended.

'Hmm,' he said at last. 'I'm not sure.'

'Not sure I pass muster?'

'No, I'm not sure it's the girl I remember. You're different.'

'You don't remember that girl at all,' she said with cool irony. 'You forgot her the next day.'

He made a face. 'Some women linger longer than others. I recall some things about her. She was a cheeky imp, always ready with a smart answer.'

'Oh, that's me. Definitely. As you'll find out if you try to get clever.'

'Ah! And "getting clever" means—?'

'Anything I want it to mean. I'm like that. Awkward.'

'Good. That's how a woman should be. I don't like the compliant, submissive kind.'

'Oh, please! Who do you think you're kidding? The compliant, submissive kind is all you have time for.'

'No, no—that's just the public image.'

'Yeah, right!'

He grinned. 'I'm not as bad as I'm painted, honestly.'

'Don't let your admirers suspect that,' she said coolly. 'They like to think you're worse than you're painted. If you start coming across as a decent fellow it could cost you a fortune in sponsorships.'

'Ah, yes, macho is better.' He struck his forehead. 'I must try to remember how to do that. I'm sure I've got a book about it somewhere.'

'You probably wrote it.'

'You see too much,' he said. 'I'm afraid of you.'

'That's better.' She struck an attitude, declaiming, 'Fear is good. Fear is what I like. Fear is constructive.'

He edged away. 'I'm getting more scared by the minute.'

She raised her plastic cup to him, sipped the wine, then rose and strolled slowly away. She needed to set a distance between them until she was more certain of her control.

She was shocked at herself. She'd meant to be so level-headed—a responsible citizen and devoted mother, efficient, practical. Part of her was managing that, but the other part was like a dazzled teenager on her first date.

But in some ways he *was* her first date—then and now. Over the years she'd been out with other men, but nothing had come of it because no man could touch her heart.

Then this one man had had come bursting out of the shadows, reminding her of how easily he'd conquered that very heart once, and how fatal it would be to let him do it again.

She must play him cleverly; drawing him close for Mike's sake, but protecting her inner self. An excitement was rising in her, but she beat it down. Control. Common sense.

Right! She had it now.

'Stop just there,' he called.

She did so, half turning to find him leaning back on the bench, enjoying the view.

'You're definitely not her,' he said. 'She was a skinny little thing, no curves. Now, *you*—'

'The odd curve or two,' she agreed. 'I owe that to Mike.

There's nothing like having a baby to make you go in and out.'

Now, she thought, he would ask about Mike. Surely it must occur to him to wonder—especially about the name? But, if so, he was keeping it to himself.

'Then I reckon I have to give in and admit that it's really you,' he said.

'Disappointed?' she asked.

'No,' he said softly, and suddenly the humour was gone from his voice, and from his eyes, leaving only intensity. Just one word, but the world had changed.

'Come back,' he said, taking her hand and leading her back to the bench. 'No, wait—you're cold.'

'I'm fine,' she said, although she was beginning to feel the breeze.

'No, you're not. Here.' Removing his jacket, he slipped it around her shoulders and gave her a brief squeeze. 'Shall we find somewhere indoors?'

'No,' she said quickly. 'It's nice out here. I come here sometimes to enjoy the peace.'

'I expect Mike likes to play here with other kids.'

'Not really. He enjoys noisy games, where he can shout at the top of his voice.'

'Ah, yes. I remember that feeling.'

She thought of the clamour that had always been part of his life—not just engines, but people. He was a natural talker, and liked to surround himself with folk who had plenty to say. It was almost as though he feared the silence.

But now she saw him leaning back, his face raised to the sky, eyes closed, his expression suggesting deep satisfaction—like a man enjoying a rare pleasure.

He opened his eyes.

'It's beautiful,' he said softly. 'Usually I don't get anything like this.'

'Yes, your life has always been noisy.'

Did she only imagine that he gave a faint shudder?

'Noise, noise, noise,' he murmured. 'Once I was fine with it. Now it seems to beat on me. I've even thought—sometimes— what am I doing? There's got to be more to life.'

'You mean give up racing and do something else?'

'Well, I could always be a cab driver,' he said significantly.

So he *did* remember that evening—right down to a daft little joke they'd exchanged.

'You'd be a rotten cab driver. Everything would have to be done your way.'

'Of course,' he said, theatrically lofty, 'because I'm always right.'

'Yes, I do remember that much about you,' she agreed. 'It's how you always win.'

'I don't always win,' he murmured.

He spoke so quietly that she wondered if she'd been meant to hear at all.

'You do according to Mike,' she said. 'He's your biggest fan. Thank you for being so nice to him.'

'He's a great kid. You must be very proud of him.'

'Yes, I am.'

Now he would ask her about Mike—who had fathered him, what had happened in her life since that night. But he said nothing, and she stared, becoming increasingly puzzled.

But perhaps it wasn't so surprising that Jared couldn't see that Mike was his. There was no likeness. Jared's hair and eyes were both dark, his face lean and tense. Mike's hair was fair, his eyes blue, his face chubby. Their only resemblance lay in the hint of wickedness in their eyes. But how could he see that?

'Perhaps we should be going back,' he said, and she wondered at the note of unease in his voice.

'Yes, I mustn't be away too long.'

Slowly they made their way back along the path that led to the street. What should she do next? she wondered. This might be her one chance to tell him about Mike. Shouldn't she take it, risking his indifference? Or, worse than indifference, hostility. But at least then she would know where she stood.

She took a deep breath. 'The fact is—' She stopped suddenly, staring ahead.

'What's the matter?' he asked.

'There.' She pointed through the trees to where they could just see her home across the road. 'The light's come on in Mike's bedroom. He gets bad dreams sometimes. I'd better go and see if he's all right.'

He came too, following her into the house just as Sam was climbing the stairs with a glass of milk.

'Is he all right?' Kaye asked.

'I think so. We heard him calling in his sleep and went in. He says he's just thirsty.'

'He won't ever admit to having bad dreams,' Kaye sighed.

'He probably thinks they're for wimps,' Jared said.

They all looked up as Mike came flying out onto the landing, glaring down the stairs at them, astounded at the sight of Jared.

'I'm not having nightmares,' he cried. 'I'm not, I'm not.'

'All right, all right,' Jared said easily. 'If you say so.'

He moved a few steps up, meeting Mike who had descended far enough to glare at him.

'I'm *not.*'

'Then you're luckier than I am,' Jared said, sitting on the stairs as though this was the most natural thing in the world. 'Boy, you should see some of my dreams. Real nightmares.'

'You?' Mike stared, not really believing what he'd just heard.

'Sure. Sit down.' He moved over so that Mike could settle beside him. Down below the others kept silent, watching and holding their breaths.

'Sometimes my job's dangerous,' Jared said. 'That can be the most fun, but you need to find a way of coping. Dreams can help.'

'Help?'

'You relive it in your sleep, and sometimes you wake up knowing that you've been through the worst. Or at least knowing what you should do.'

'I don't do dangerous things,' Mike protested. 'But I—' He stopped cautiously.

'But you still have the odd shouting match with yourself when you're asleep? We all do sometimes.' Jared's tone became confiding. 'It happened to me a lot when I was a kid, because I began to understand that I couldn't always make the world do what I wanted.'

'But the world does everything you want now,' Mike said.

'Mmm, sometimes. Now and then you have to compromise. For instance, I'm planning to take your mother out tomorrow night, but she hasn't agreed yet so I'm counting on you to help the negotiations.'

'Mum!' Mike squeaked, outraged.

'Yes, darling.'

'Why didn't you say yes?'

'Because I haven't been asked yet,' she said, glaring at Jared.

'Oh, did I forget that detail?' he asked innocently. 'I can't think why.'

'I can,' she said, torn between indignation and amusement. 'It was the quickest way of making me dance to your tune.'

'Yeah, that must have been it,' he mused. 'Well, how about it, Mike? Do I have your permission?'

'What about *my* permission?' Kaye demanded.

'I'll leave this to you,' Jared told Mike with a wink.

Mike nodded. 'Don't worry. She'll be there. Promise.'

'When the two of you have finished telling me what to do...' Kaye observed.

Neither of them took any notice of her. They were too busy shaking hands.

'I think you should go back to bed now,' she told Mike.

'Promise,' he demanded.

'Now, look—'

'Promise or I won't go back to bed.'

She glanced up at Jared. 'Then I'll have to—but only to please Mike.'

'That's understood,' he said solemnly.

'Bed,' Ethel commanded Mike.

He nodded and put his hand in hers. Having got his own way he was as docile as a lamb.

Kaye showed Jared to the door.

'Sorry to do it like that,' he said, 'but I need to get you to myself. We have a lot to talk about.'

She nodded. 'Yes, we do.'

'I'll call for you tomorrow night, at seven.'

'Good. Then you'll be in time to help me put Mike to bed. He'd never forgive us if you didn't.'

'That's what I hoped,' he said quietly.

He touched her face with gentle fingertips. Then he was gone, walking away through the park.

Kaye almost closed the front door, but kept it open just a crack while she watched him vanish into the darkness. One question had been answered. A hundred more still remained. But the sudden peace and contentment in her heart were overwhelming.

Later that night, in his hotel room, Jared threw himself on the bed, staring up at the ceiling, trying to come to terms with the evening. In one way it had been just as he expected. In another it had been a stunning surprise.

He'd known Kaye would be changed, but he'd been unprepared for what he'd found: a woman with sad eyes and a way of withdrawing into herself without warning. She retained the wit of her younger days, but she was no longer light-hearted. Instead there was an air of haunting mystery that had never been there before.

His fault? Almost certainly. He must find out and comfort her, if she would let him. Perhaps her barricades were there to exclude him most of all? And could he blame her? No. He must accept the blame as his own.

Another new experience.

But the biggest shock had been Mike. Sitting on the stairs, reaching out to the child by sharing things they had in common, realising that they were one in mind and perhaps in heart— nothing in his life had prepared him for that. If this dazzling little boy turned out not to be his he would be bitterly disappointed.

But he had no fear of that.

From his pocket he took a small photograph of a pretty girl with a rounded face, fair hair and blue eyes. It was his own mother, taken when she was young.

In Jared's mind Mike appeared beside the girl. He gave a sigh of satisfaction. The same face. No doubt of it.

Now he knew what he'd come to find out, and the way ahead was as clear as a racetrack, with the chequered flag in sight.

CHAPTER THREE

NEXT day he texted.

Glad rags tonight. J.

She texted back.

Shame. I was going to try out a new helmet. K.

His message came back.

Me too. J.

By seven o'clock she was ready, in a dress of deep blue that brought out the depths of her eyes, and her hair had been arranged in a clever combination of elegant and casual. Hell would freeze over before she let Jared suspect she'd taken trouble about her appearance. Even though she had.

'You'll knock his eyes out,' Ethel said with satisfaction. 'He'll wonder how he stayed away from you for so long.'

'That's not the idea,' Kaye protested untruthfully.

'Isn't it? You're not human, then.'

'It's for Mike's sake. He needs his father and I'm going to make sure they get to know each other. Nothing more.'

Ethel nodded wisely. 'Well done, darling. You keep telling yourself that.'

The doorbell rang before she could think of a reply.

'I'm not late, am I?' Jared asked, smiling.

'Bang on time.'

'Mum, is that him?' Mike's voice came from upstairs and his face could be seen through the banisters.

'Right here,' Jared called, bounding up the stairs.

Their voices dropped. Mike seemed to be doing most of the talking. Kaye just heard, 'She doesn't like—' and Jared's reply, 'I'll remember that.' Plainly Mike was giving his instructions and Jared was taking mental notes.

At last Jared said, 'I'd better go now.'

'Yes—don't keep her waiting,' Mike advised solemnly. 'She gets mad.'

'Oi, cheeky!' Kaye called up the stairs, and was rewarded with two male guffaws.

'Goodnight, Mike,' she said, climbing the stairs to reach him. 'Go to bed, go to sleep, and stop organising my life.'

'That's the trouble with women,' Jared confided to the child. 'They need us to organise them, but they won't admit it.'

Mike nodded. They shook hands.

'Bed,' Kaye said firmly, kissing him.

'Night.' He kissed her and vanished into his room, from whence came the sound of giggling.

'Let's go before I get into any more trouble,' Jared said hurriedly.

Outside, he had a taxi waiting to take them to a restaurant whose plain exterior belied the luxury within. A waiter led them to a table in a discreet corner and hovered to take their order for aperitifs. Jared consulted her taste, giving the matter his whole attention—as he did everything in life, Kaye realised.

Disconcertingly, it served to antagonise her again, as she recalled a hundred newspaper tales of glamorous women he'd escorted, wining and dining them just like this, while she'd been left alone, struggling to raise the son he neither knew about nor wanted to know about.

When the waiter had departed Jared leaned back in his seat, grinning.

'I need this drink,' he said. 'Mike doesn't let you get away with anything, does he?'

'I'm sorry if he made you nervous,' Kaye said.

'I reckon he's always going to make people nervous, because he seems to get one step ahead. What a great kid!'

'Yes, he is,' she said eagerly.

Tonight she must tell him that he had a son. If he rejected that, she would manage somehow. After all, rejection was what she was used to. But Jared seemed drawn to the child, and perhaps Mike could really have a father. Only he mattered.

To prepare the ground, she continued, 'The teachers tell me he's advanced for his age. He's only five, but he's already starting to read and write. He's good at drawing, a dab hand on a computer, and he's got this great outgoing personality. I envy him that.'

'Don't you have an outgoing personality?' he asked with a touch of surprise.

'Not really. Sometimes yes; sometimes no. My wary side can take over. But he doesn't seem to have a wary side.'

'Tell me about it.' Jared grinned.

'He's got no sense of fear. It makes me want to protect him, but then he gets so cross.'

He nodded. 'I can imagine. I've always been the same. In fact I—'

'What is it?' she asked, for he seemed suddenly uneasy.

'Last night—I should apologise, shouldn't I?'

'What for?'

'Well—Mike—'

'But you were wonderful with Mike. You told him just what he needed to hear. If his hero has bad dreams too then it isn't sissy, is it? Why would you apologise for that?'

'Thanks—I'm glad if I helped. But—well—' He was floundering. He seldom apologised to anyone about anything, unless it was the kind of light-hearted 'sorry' he'd give Hal after a race. But this apology mattered. Mike mattered. *She* mattered.

'I did rather take him over, didn't I?' he managed to say at last. 'You're his mother, but I didn't give you a chance. Why are you smiling?'

'At how easily fooled you are,' she said in delight.

'What do you mean?'

'Jared, you didn't take Mike over. He took *you* over.'

He stared. 'Yes, I guess he did at that.'

'What he wants he just goes for. You, me, Sam and Ethel, the kids at school, even the teachers sometimes. We all end up dancing to his tune.'

Jared gave a rueful grin. 'I guess I just fell into line. That's all right—as long as you weren't upset.'

She shook her head. 'You made him happy, and that's all I care about.'

'All?' he asked casually, not looking at her.

'I'm a parent. My baby comes first. It goes with the territory.' The moment had come. She took a deep breath and added quietly, 'I guess you know why I'm saying that.'

She half expected him to flinch away, play dumb, but she had underestimated him. He met her eyes, defenceless. 'It's true, then? He's mine?'

'Yes,' she said simply.

'Mine—my son.'

Although he must have suspected the truth it still seemed to bewilder him. He repeated the words in a daze, as though trying to understand them.

'My child—' he whispered. 'He's my child—mine.'

Suddenly he dropped his head into his hands. Across the narrow table Kaye could see him shaking and was strangely invaded by pity.

'Jared,' she murmured, reaching out to him. 'It's all right.'

As soon as he felt the touch of her fingers he seized them in a terrible grip, not raising his head but shaking it from side

to side like a man in a state of confusion. She reached out her
other hand, caressing what little she could see of his face.

'It's all right,' she repeated. She wasn't quite sure what she
meant by the words, except to convey a message of warmth and
reassurance.

'It's not all right,' he groaned, raising his head. 'How could
I have been such a fool? When we parted that night I was sure
that I'd been careful—but that was just me being stupid and
ignorant. You were so young and innocent—a virgin—and I
couldn't face my own guilt. I told myself you'd get in touch if
anything went wrong, and when you didn't I thought all was
well. Kaye, why didn't you tell me? Did you hate me?'

'No, of course not. I tried to contact you, but by the time I
suspected I was pregnant you'd left the firm and you weren't
easy to get in touch with. It was like a wall had come down
around you. I sent a text to your cell phone and got back a
message saying, *'Thank you for contacting Jared Marriot.
This number is now closed, but he thanks you for your good
wishes.'*

Jared closed his eyes, as though seeking refuge from the
terrible truth, or perhaps from himself. Kaye, still holding his
hand, gave it a little squeeze.

'I think that was Mirella,' he said. 'We were getting close,
but she tried to manipulate me even closer. I broke it off because she went too far, tried to keep people away, but I never
realised how far she'd gone. But it's still my fault. I should have
contacted you. I should have—'

'Hush,' she said gently. 'It's long ago. We were both
younger—'

'And I was stupid and selfish. Why did you let me get away
with it? You might have sued me for support—showed me up
for the world to jeer at—'

'But they wouldn't have jeered at you,' she said wryly. 'Just
me, for being rejected.'

'I didn't reject you,' he said with soft violence. 'Call me
immature, irresponsible, half-witted—'

'If you really want me to,' she said with a slight smile. 'Anything you say.'

'I deserve it. I deserve everything bad you could say or do.' He checked himself and sighed. 'But that wouldn't help, would it? I'm floundering around, not facing things, just as I did then. You're the one who's had all the problems.'

'And all the happiness,' she reminded him. 'I've had five years of watching Mike grow, learn to walk and talk, discovering how bright he is. You've missed all that. I reckon I'm the lucky one.'

'But you were left to raise him without any help from me. I wasn't there when you gave birth. I've never been there when it mattered. Don't make it easy for me, Kaye. Even with Sam and Ethel you must have been lonely.'

'Sometimes, yes. Sometimes, no.'

'Any—particular friends?'

She guessed he was angling to find out about boyfriends, but she wasn't going to make it that easy for him.

'They come and go,' she said vaguely. 'I don't tend to lay out the welcome mat.'

'No, I can imagine. But I still don't understand why you didn't pursue me and make me face my responsibilities.'

'I was afraid you wouldn't believe me. Or you might have pressured me to end the pregnancy—'

'Would you have done that?'

How could he dare to ask that? she wondered. She could never have destroyed the child that she carried, but especially not *his* child—the child of a man who'd touched her heart, even though their time together had been brief. What had happened to her that night had stayed a part of her—not just in her pregnancy, but in the way her spirit had clung to him ever since. But clearly this was something he couldn't or wouldn't understand. Her antagonism flared again.

'No,' she said quietly. 'I wouldn't have done that.'

'Are you angry with me for asking?'

'A bit. You see—'

'There are a million things I still have to learn,' he said, winning her sympathy again with his understanding. 'I'm going to have to let you lead the way along this path. That is, if you want to?'

'I want to,' she whispered.

'Every step of the way—wherever it leads. And that's what we don't know. Do you remember how I was? Always cock-a-hoop, sure I knew everything.'

'Yes, I remember that,' she said tenderly.

He grimaced. 'And then things happen that take you by surprise.'

'But perhaps you shouldn't be surprised,' she pointed out lightly. 'The life you've led—Mike probably isn't the only one. Careful!'

His glass had slipped from his hand and smashed onto the floor. Waiters hurried over to clear up the broken glass and replace the wine.

'Sorry about that,' he said tensely when there was peace again. 'There aren't any others. I'd have known. No other girl would have let me get away with it as you did.' He saw her faint frown and hastened to add, 'You think you're one of a crowd? You're wrong. You're special. I knew it even then, but—'

'But things were different then, weren't they?' she asked gently.

'What do you mean by that?' he asked quickly.

'Nothing,' she said, puzzled by a hint of sharpness in his voice.

'You must have meant something. Different how?'

'We were different people. The years have changed us, made us grow up. You were only twenty-four, and most lads of that age aren't ready for responsibility.'

Did she only imagine that he relaxed, as though with relief?

'Yes, I was just a kid in those days,' he said. 'There was a lot I wasn't ready for.'

His face was wary, uncertain, as though he feared that every step might be the one that destroyed his dreams. She'd never seen such a look from him before.

'We still have a thousand things to talk about,' he said. 'But not here and now. I want to be alone with you for a long time, with no interruptions.'

'Yes,' she said quietly. She knew a sense of relief. She'd sensed, as he had, that this wasn't the moment to go any further. 'Time without interruptions isn't easy to come by if you're a racing driver.'

'Right. A different country every two weeks or so. Tomorrow I leave for Spain. Hell! But when I come back you'll still be here, won't you?' His voice was tense again.

'Yes, I'll be here.' A thought struck her. 'Are you on the early flight tomorrow?'

'Yes.'

'Then it's time you were home and in bed.'

'Bullying me, huh?'

'No, I'm just thinking of Mike. If you're not at your best and don't win the race I'll have a lot of explaining to do. Come along. Get going.'

'Yes, nanny!' he said with teasing obedience. 'You sound like my mother. The night before my first Grand Prix she ordered me to bed as though I was five.'

'I guess she understood you well. Come along.'

He'd said he liked to be in charge at all times, but he seemed happy enough to follow her lead now.

In the taxi, he said, 'Suddenly I don't want to go to Spain.'

'Oh, yes, you do,' she said lightly. 'Racing comes first.'

He grimaced. 'Does it? Well, if you say so. What's that smile for?'

'I've just realised what a problem I'm going to have over the next few days. My team is Brent, but secretly I'll be rooting for you.'

'Promise me that's true.'

'I promise,' she said softly.

'And when I return we'll meet up on the first day?'

'Are you kidding? Mike would never forgive me if we didn't.'

'I'm not talking about Mike now.'

As the taxi drew up outside her home she prevented him coming with her to the door.

'Go home,' she said. 'Get some sleep.'

'Whatever you say.' He kissed her cheek.

'Goodnight,' she said. And fled.

Mike was sleeping when she looked in on him, and she quietly retreated to her own room. It had been a good evening. Jared had accepted his son more easily than she'd dared to hope, and she could feel him reaching out to herself.

Yet she was pervaded by a sense of alarm. She'd told him that the years had changed them, making them different people, and it was true. They had both become more mature—especially Jared. But there was another change in herself.

When she looked back on the girl she'd been then—open-hearted, open-armed, ready to love and embrace the world—she could hardly believe that she was the same person.

She'd borne a child to a man who'd simply brushed her aside, and it had changed her beyond recognition. Now she was suspicious, where once she'd been trusting, withdrawn where she'd been eager. The girl who'd once been filled with hope had learned to expect the worst.

Her own reaction to Jared's return had surprised and worried her. She hadn't rushed into his arms, she reassured herself, but she'd brushed hard-won caution aside far too easily.

A warning voice was sounding in her head.

Beware. Hold back. He wants his child, but does he want you? Don't throw away the painful lessons you've learned just because he smiles at you.

She looked out of the window at the park where they had walked the night before, as though she might find some kind of answer in its depths. But there was only the darkness, the soft rustling of the trees, and no answer in the whole universe.

* * *

When she arrived at work next morning, the owner of Brent, Mr Salcombe, was waiting for her, his face dark and angry.

'What did you think you were doing?' he snapped.

'When?'

'Last night. You were seen with Jared Marriott, with your heads very close together. Cannonball would give anything to learn the secret of our new gearbox, and now I suppose they know *everything*.'

The mere thought of being with Jared and wasting time discussing gearboxes was so outrageous that she had to choke back a laugh.

'Very funny,' her boss snapped. 'I won't tolerate disloyalty. Clear your desk and go.'

'But—'

'*Go!*'

It was all over that fast. Within an hour she was outside the building, minus a job. She texted Jared, telling him what had happened, and awaited his reply.

It didn't come.

She sent another text, worded more urgently.

Silence.

Nightmares danced about her. It was happening again. He'd simply chosen to disappear.

She could have laughed at her own stupidity in ever believing in him. She'd feared that he might try to seduce her to get close to Mike, but he wasn't even bothering with that.

Sam and Ethel looked up in alarm as she stormed home.

'That's it,' she said. 'I can forget any sentimental ideas I may have had.'

Briefly she described what had happened.

'And when I try to contact him he's just vanished again,' she finished. 'So now I know.'

'You're too ready to look on the dark side,' Sam insisted.

'Well, maybe the dark side is safer. I knew that before. I should have stuck to it.'

'But he won't just dump you if he wants to stay in touch with Mike,' Ethel pointed out.

'Oh, he wants his son, all right. But there are lawyers for that.'

At the word 'lawyers' she sensed a frisson go through her grandparents.

'What is it?'

'Just before you came home there was phone call from a firm of lawyers,' Ethel said. 'They asked for your e-mail address. Oh, dear!'

'Well, at least I've been warned,' Kaye said through gritted teeth. 'Let's have a look.'

The e-mail was already there, its message conveyed in plain, uncompromising terms.

Mr. Marriot is employing us to handle details of the financial situation between him and yourself concerning his son. He proposes a monthly fee for future support, and a lump sum to cover the previous five years. The amounts he suggests are—

'Wow!' Sam breathed, reading over her shoulder. 'That is one helluva lot of money.'

'Of course it is,' Kaye said bitterly. 'In return he expects to get Mike without trouble. His son is his property, you see, and he doesn't want me to make difficulties. Oh, boy, is he in for a shock!'

Her voice sounded controlled, but inwardly she was screaming. She'd believed him. She'd even come to the verge of trusting him—a notable journey for her. And all the time *this* had been the underlying truth.

Her phone rang. She snatched it up, ready to unleash her bitterness on Jared, but she heard an unfamiliar female voice.

'Ms Linton? I'm calling from Team Cannonball. I was given your number by Mr Marriot. We urgently need to hire someone who can speak several languages, and he says you would be ideal.'

'Mr Marriot—said that?'

'He praised you in the highest terms, and he seemed to think you might be available.'

'I—well, I don't have a job at the moment.'

'Excellent. Everyone is in Spain for the Grand Prix, and Mr Vanner, our managing director, would like to meet you. Can you travel today?'

'Yes—yes.'

'Splendid! I'll arrange your tickets and accommodation.'

She hung up, leaving Kaye in a whirl. Now she had no idea *what* to think. With one hand Jared seemed to push her away; with the other he invited her in. Hope was flowering anew. But she couldn't believe it. She didn't want to believe it. Trust was too dangerous.

The phone rang. This time it was him.

'I told them you were the best,' he said, adding as an after-thought, 'Spanish *is* one of your languages, isn't it?'

'Luckily, yes.'

'Phew. That was a near thing. We'll meet up later today.'

'Jared—wait—'

'We'll talk tonight,' he said, and hung up with a speed that might have led a suspicious person to think he was avoiding certain subjects. As for whether Kaye actually was that suspicious person, even she was no longer sure.

'You see—you were wrong,' Ethel said. 'He's not dumping you. Don't judge people so quickly.'

'Is that what I am? Judgemental?'

'It's not your fault, but you're too ready to expect the worst, and the worst doesn't always happen. Try to keep a more open mind, otherwise you could spoil your own life.'

Kaye kissed her. 'Bless you. I'll try to remember.'

The two of them, and Mike, came to the airport with her. Mike was sulking at not being allowed to come too, but at the last minute he relented and pressed a drawing into her hand.

'I did it for him,' he said. 'Promise to give it to him.'

'I promise, darling.'

'Will passengers for Valencia please—?'

A round of kisses and she was on her way. During the flight she studied the sketch, which showed a racing car with a helmeted driver waving both hands above his head. It was childish, but skilled for his age, and she looked forward to Jared's reaction.

Her own feelings were in a state of confusion. Only a few hours ago he'd seemed to have turned his back on her, inspiring in her a resentment that had been almost hatred. But then he'd persuaded his team to employ her and bring her to his side. On the telephone his voice had been friendly, but with an undercurrent of tension that kept her caution alive.

She must cling to that caution, she warned herself. Her heart might urge her to yield, but it was her mind that ruled these days. She wondered who would meet her at the airport. Not Jared himself. He would be far too busy preparing for the race.

But he was there, waiting as she came though Customs, and when he saw her he waved his hands above his head exactly as he did when he won a race—and as the sketch showed. But of course, sang the voice in her heart, refusing to be silenced a moment longer. Of *course* he'd come for her himself—just as secretly she had always known that he would.

But joy must wait just a little longer. There was a man with him who turned out to be Mr Vanner, the boss. Too impress him, Kaye put on a show, talking to officials in perfect Spanish, and she saw him relax and nod.

'OK, I'm satisfied,' he said. 'We'll talk money later. Now I'll be off. I'm sure you two don't need me.'

'You bet we don't,' Jared murmured in her ear as he led her to a taxi.

As soon as the car started her pulled her into his arms. Years had passed since their last real kiss, and now she knew she'd longed for this from the first moment of his return. The feel of his lips against hers was like returning to life after a long sleep, and the life she rediscovered was glorious. There were so many things they must still discuss, but none of them mattered beside what was happening to her now, and the new person she was becoming.

All too soon they reached the hotel, returning reluctantly to the real world. They must climb out, speaking and acting normally until Kaye had been shown to her room and the door had closed on the porter.

He took a step forward. 'I was so afraid you wouldn't come.'

'I can't believe this happened,' she murmured. 'Those lawyers—money—'

'But of course. I should have been supporting the two of you already, so it's only right to make up for it.'

'I wish you'd told me that earlier. I thought—'

He stared. 'Thought what?'

'All that talk of money—' She took a deep breath and said in a shaking voice, 'I didn't think I'd see you again.'

'You thought I was trying to buy you off?' he said, aghast. 'Just claiming my fatherly rights and keeping you at a distance? How could you—?' But he checked himself with a groan. 'No, of course you thought that. It's my fault for being so clumsy. I did it all in a rush—calling the lawyers from the airport as I was getting ready to board. I should have told you first. Kaye, I swear to you, this isn't about money.'

She gave him a long, heart-searching look, knowing that at last it had come: the moment for which she'd waited years. 'Isn't it?' she murmured. 'You may have to convince me.'

A faint, self-mocking smile illuminated his face as he reached for her, whispering, 'I think I'll enjoy doing that.' His hands became more possessive as he drew her closer. 'Let me show you what it really is about.'

CHAPTER FOUR

AFTERWARDS she slept in his arms in a state of peace that she hadn't known for years. She'd made love not only with her body, but with her heart and soul—something she had never thought to do. But it had felt right. The wariness and mistrust had released her, like bonds falling away, and suddenly everything about being with Jared felt right.

Waking, she lay curled up against him, trying to remember how things had been earlier that same day, when she'd believed he'd rejected her again. Now she seemed to have stepped into another universe.

'What's that sigh for?' he asked.

'I was just thinking about the way things happen. You just can't plan for anything, can you? When I woke up this morning I worked for Brent. Then I go in, get fired, and now I'm working for Cannonball.'

'It's fate,' he said. 'That's what it is.'

'It must be—otherwise it would be scary to think what a big part chance plays in life. Who could have predicted that someone would see us together and tell Salcombe that I must be passing on secrets?'

His head turned slightly, and she looked up to find him regarding her with wry humour.

'What is it?' she asked, as some inkling of the incredible truth began to dawn on her. *'Jared, what did you do?'*

'Let's just say I don't believe in leaving things to chance.'

'You—are you telling me—?'

'Actually, I'm trying not to tell you, because I'm not ready to die,' he said, looking warily at her face.

'You *fixed* it,' she breathed.

'I arranged for someone to pass certain information on to Salcombe.'

'And got me fired?'

'It was necessary.'

'Why? I could have given in my notice.'

'That would have taken weeks. I wanted you today.'

'You scheming, manipulative, devious, conniving—'

'I prefer Machiavellian. It's more dignified. Hey, don't hit me.'

Laughing, he dodged her flying hands, which were slapping him nineteen to the dozen.

'I should do more than hit you,' she seethed. 'How dare you simply organise my life to suit yourself, without asking what I wanted?'

'But it's simpler that way,' he declared, with an air of innocence that made her fight back her own laughter. 'You might not have wanted the same as I wanted, and then what would I have done?'

'Backed off? Given up?'

'Oh, no, I never do that,' he said solemnly. 'If I want something, I take it. Always in charge. Always in the driving seat. That's me.'

There was mischief in his eyes, but also a warning. This was how he was. Take it or leave it. He would use any means to get what he wanted. Only yesterday she would have taken warning from that, and blamed him. But in this new world where she found herself she only saw that what he wanted was herself.

Overjoyed, she ignored the warning and threw herself back into his arms.

That night was the happiest of her life.

* * *

Next morning she awoke to find herself alone, Jared having slipped back to his own room. The press was out in force, and they would have to be careful. After breakfast with the team her day would be spent at the track.

They met briefly going down the stairs, and she seized the chance to show him Mike's picture.

'I meant to give it to you as soon as we met,' she said. 'But—er—'

'But we got distracted,' he supplied wryly. 'Hey, this is great.'

'I told you he was an artist.'

'As well as a computer genius. What a kid. Just a minute.'

He whipped out his cell phone, dialled, and a moment later his face lit up.

'Mike? Great to talk to you. That picture—wonderful. Did you really do it yourself? I can't believe it.'

He went on in this way for five minutes, while Mike squealed his pleasure so loud that Kaye heard it.

'I'll hand you over to your mum now,' Jared said at last. 'But don't keep her long. We have to get to the track.'

She could have hugged Jared for the way he'd accepted Mike right from the start. He was going to be a wonderful father. She felt that her happiness was surely too great to be real. But it *was* real. That was the best of all.

Now all his thoughts were of the race, but it was enough to be near him, knowing that he wanted her there. She made herself useful to Mr Vanner in the background, not wanting to distract Jared from the coming danger.

There were three vital days. First came the practice sessions, when the drivers could study the track, making notes about bends and straights, where it was good to overtake, where overtaking should be avoided at all costs. Following that there would be work done on the cars so that they could perform at their best on that particular track, and next day came the qualifying sessions, when the drivers raced around the circuit—the fastest being awarded 'pole position' at the front of the starting grid.

In Team Cannonball there were a few nerves. As the current world champion Jared was expected to get pole position, but on the last race he'd lost it to Hal. He'd won that race, but nobody was going to feel at ease until he'd qualified at the front. Least of all Jared himself.

But everything went well. In practice he stormed ahead, his qualifying lap was fastest, and he achieved pole position. On the night before the race he retired early, blissfully happy.

'Tomorrow's going to be a good day,' he murmured sleepily.

'Just be careful,' she urged. 'Please be careful.'

'Careful? That's not what it's about.'

'But Jared—Jared—?'

He was already asleep.

He didn't know what she was talking about, she realised. Caution? What was that? The risks he took were calculated to the extreme degree, and as far as he was concerned that was all that mattered.

But now she was living in a different world, one that shrieked DANGER when he got into the car.

She tried to be reasonable. Everything was safer now. Drivers crashed, but got out of their cars and walked away. It was a long time since anyone had been killed.

She thought of the last few years, when she'd watched a hundred Grand Prix on television, feeling only the calm interest of one who knew the industry from the inside. Jared had never been hers, and the feeling of distance had protected her from fear.

But now everything was different. With every hour she was growing closer to him, perhaps loving him, and was devastated at the thought of his death. She turned and lay beside him, trying to see his sleeping face but not quite managing it. He was oblivious to her, lost in the only world that would matter to him for the next few hours. She leaned over and kissed him, just managing to touch his ear.

'Come back to me,' she whispered. 'And to Mike. Don't leave

him, whatever you do. He couldn't bear it now—any more than I could.'

Then she turned over, knowing there was no more to say. She wouldn't mention the subject tomorrow, because the worst thing she could do was nag him before a race.

In the event her worries seemed groundless. Jared held the lead from start to finish. At first Kaye held her breath, her heart pounding, but Jared's mastery soon became so clear that she was able to relax until he crossed the finishing line.

She rejoiced in his victory, but what warmed her heart most was the fact that he took the first opportunity to call Mike, and talked to him for ten minutes before handing the phone to Kaye.

'Now we'll have a month without travelling,' Jared said as they lay together that night.

He was referring to the fact that the next race, in two weeks' time, was at Silverstone, in England, and she hastened to say, 'You know what Mike's going to want, don't you?'

'Yes. He'd never forgive either of us if he didn't get a visit to Silverstone. I'll fix it. I want to get to know him well before we say anything.'

'Tell him who you are, you mean? You could tell him now. He's such a fan of yours that he'll be thrilled.'

'He's a fan of the driver. I want him to be a fan of the father. Please, Kaye, humour me in this.' His eyes suddenly held a mysteriously distant look. 'It's important.'

'Of course,' she said. 'We'll tell him together when the time comes.'

It was another reason for happiness. She hadn't expected such insight from Jared.

As before, he fell asleep first—which must be natural, she realised, in a man who lived though his senses. She guessed that recent events had brought about the first hint of a change, and the discovery of his son had made him think seriously for the first time in his life. But he was still ruled by instinctive reactions.

And so am I, she mused. How many times have we made love? And did I take precautions? It never crossed my mind any more than it seems to have crossed his. And if I become pregnant again? Is that what I secretly want? Is it what he secretly wants? Is he hoping I won't notice that we aren't being careful?

A faint, daring smile illuminated her face.

Fine, she thought. Then I won't notice.

And might it not be best like this? Perhaps there was something to be said for trusting Fate to show you the way.

On the journey home next day he could talk of nothing but how much he was looking forward to being with Mike in the school holidays.

A funfair had arrived in the local park and Jared seized his chance. An evening spent with thrill rides, dodgems, big wheel and rollercoaster was exactly what the two daredevils needed to bond with each other.

Sam and Ethel came too, but went off in a different direction.

'The stalls are quite exciting enough for us,' Ethel said. 'See you later.'

Kaye never forgot that first ride on the rollercoaster—climbing slowly up into the sky, the moment at the very top with nothing between them and the heavens, then the headlong plunge. It was like her life now, she thought. Glorious heights, the descents, then climbing again, and finally coming to rest.

'Again,' Mike demanded when they landed.

'Aren't you scared?' she demanded.

His puzzled look answered her. What on earth did 'scared' mean?

She went up three more times, then persuaded her crazy menfolk to get out and head for the hoopla stall. But after a few throws Mike was determined to return to the rollercoaster.

'If you don't like it, Mummy, you don't need to come,' he said kindly.

'That's very nice of you, darling.'

Suddenly Mike threw his arms around her. 'I don't want you to be scared or upset.'

'As long as you're safe I'll be fine.'

They drew back, smiling into each other's eyes in perfect understanding. For a moment they both forgot about Jared, watching them with the gentle, quizzical expression of a man who'd just made a stunning discovery.

The moment passed quickly. A boy of five could only allow himself to be soppy for a brief time. As if to make up for it, Mike seized Jared's hand in both his, hauling him away. Jared threw Kaye a helpless look and allowed himself to be commandeered.

'I'll bet Jared was exactly like that at his age,' Ethel said from behind Kaye, where she and Sam had just appeared.

'I'm sure of it,' Kaye agreed. 'He's still like it now.'

They had secured the front of the rollercoaster, and from this distance she could just see them as they peaked and began the drop, yelling with delight, Jared's arms protectively around his son. As they slowed to a stop she could see an argument going on, which Jared ended by lifting Mike determinedly out.

'Time for home,' he said, when he'd greeted Sam and Ethel. 'You may not be knackered, but I am. Off with you, you monster. I'm going to take your mother to dinner.'

Mike was offended—not at being called a monster, which he thought perfectly proper, but at the suggestion that he should go home. But Sam yawned dramatically, and gave Jared a thumbs-up sign which made Kaye chuckle.

'Where are we having dinner?' she asked as they wandered away.

'My apartment,' he said, slipping an arm around her shoulders. 'It's not far.'

She was fascinated to see where he lived now—if it was any different from before.

It was an expensive apartment, yet with the same feeling of austerity and aloneness.

There was one photograph on the sideboard that caught her

attention. It showed a young woman in a bridal gown, gazing up into the eyes of her groom.

'That's my parents on their wedding day,' Jared said, 'taken just outside the church.'

'So that's where Mike gets his face from,' she murmured. 'No wonder you were so sure from the start.'

'One look at him and I knew we were family,' he agreed. 'I only wish my parents were still alive to see him.'

She looked closer. The bride's left hand was on her groom's arm, giving Kaye a clear view of a large engagement ring.

'They were so proud of that ring,' Jared said, grinning. 'My dad couldn't really afford it, but he said nothing was too good for her. She told me it took him months to pay for it. When she died he took it off her finger, gave it to me, and told me to be very careful who I gave it to. "It's got to be the right one," he said, "and I want to look her over first." Every time the press linked my name with a dolly girl he'd say, "You're not getting daft ideas about that one, I hope?"' He sighed, looking at her. 'It's a pity he died three years ago.'

She held her breath, wondering if his next words would be, *He'd have liked you.* But she was fated not to know. A knock at the door announced the arrival of supper.

'I took the precaution of ordering from the take away down the street,' he said.

The moment slipped past. If he'd been going to speak of marriage before, she knew he wouldn't do it now. But he'd come so close, so soon. She would have to be content with that.

Talk turned to money. The lawyers had been in touch again, and Jared wanted to finalise the arrangements.

'I've booked an appointment for us tomorrow, so that we can sign things,' he said.

'Really? Thanks for telling me.'

'Well, you know me and my controlling nature. And this way you're protected. If I vanish you can sue me for every penny.'

'Must you talk about money?' she complained.

'You're right. Other things are far more interesting.'

After that the meal was finished quickly, and there was the warmth, the darkness, and the sweet feeling of coming home.

At work Mr Vanner was pleased with her, the pay was good, and life slipped into a pleasant phase. Jared didn't hint again at marriage, but he arranged for them to be together as often as possible, culminating in the British Grand Prix. Both Brent and Cannonball had built their factories in the English Midlands, to be near the Silverstone track, so for once working on the race didn't involve lengthy travel.

At Jared's insistence Kaye was allowed to bring Mike for a visit to the pits, where he was treated as a celebrity. Nobody asked about his connection with Jared. Nobody needed to.

Jared drove the fastest practice lap. Second fastest were the two Brent drivers—Hal, and a newcomer called Gary who was tipped for great things. He had a mighty good opinion of himself and regarded Jared with jealousy.

'Watch out for him,' Kaye murmured. 'He's a nasty piece of work.'

'Hmm. A bit like Warrior,' Jared agreed. 'Don't worry.'

In the event he won the race without trouble, with Gary doing no more than glower.

At the party that followed, Mr Vanner murmured to Kaye, 'We're all feeling relief right now. You know Jared did badly in a lot of races at the start of the season? He fell behind on points, but recently he's been winning again, and his points are building back up. Another couple of wins and he'll regain the lead.'

There was no doubt now that Sam and Ethel were supporting them all the way. Twice they invited Jared to dinner, treating him as one of the family with a lack of caution that actually made Kaye feel awkward.

Soon, she knew, they would have to make decisions about Mike, about themselves and each other, but she was too wise to force the moment.

Then, one evening, there was a strange incident.

They were in his home, cooking together, laughing over the fact that he was the better cook.

'I remember this from before,' she said. 'You told me how your mother had taught you to cook. I'm expecting great things of this meal.'

Her expectations were fulfilled. He pulled out all the stops and fed her superbly.

'At least let me make the coffee,' she begged as they finished, and he agreed.

As she made the coffee she suddenly remembered something. The day they had met again she'd thought she saw him in the school car park and had meant to ask him about it. But with so much happening it had slipped her mind.

She must remember to ask him soon, she thought, and they would laugh together. Perhaps tonight. She glanced into the other room, and was in time to see him go to a drawer, take out a small box, extract from it his mother's ring and slip it into his pocket.

In a flash all thoughts of the car park were abandoned. He was going to propose, she thought, trying not to be overcome by excitement. The road they had been travelling together would reach its glorious destination.

As she took in the coffee, Jared's phone rang.

'Guess who?' he said. 'Mike, what a surprise!'

He gave Mike a good ten minutes before ringing off.

'He's never lost for something to say,' he observed. 'What a boy!'

'Yes, I envy other mothers whose children aren't so gorgeous,' she agreed. 'I want a dozen more, all like him. Jared? Is something the matter?'

'What?'

'You drew a sharp breath. Are you in pain?'

'Yes, I've got a bit of a headache. It came on suddenly. It happens to me sometimes and—and once they start I must go to bed.'

'I'll stay and look after you.'

'No, I need to be alone. I'll call you.'

His voice was strained and his face dreadfully pale. She hurried to leave, since that was what he wanted, but it hurt that a gap had opened up again between them. For some reason need made him turn away from her, not towards her.

It was several days before she saw him again. During that time he texted her frequently, but didn't call.

'I hope he's better soon,' Mr Vanner said worriedly. 'We're flying to Germany in a couple of days.'

But his brow cleared next morning when Jared appeared, fully recovered, pleasant and smiling. It might all never have happened.

Kaye couldn't forget how she'd been relegated to the outside, yet Jared seemed intent on making it up to her—often clasping her hand out of sight of the others, and smiling at her in a way that reminded her of the world they shared.

In Germany he achieved the fastest time in the qualifying laps, securing pole position for himself, and beating Gary into second place on the grid.

That night they dined alone and quietly. When they went to bed he didn't try to make love, but slept with his hand on her, as though afraid she would vanish.

Next day the race went well. Jared led all the way, outwitting all attempts to overtake him until the very last bend, when a sudden frisson went through the team watching on screen. Gary was trying to edge past in a highly dangerous manner.

'He's going to make Jared crash,' one of the Cannonball team said furiously. 'Trying to force him into that wall if he doesn't give way.' He seized the microphone and barked into it. *'Let him pass, man. It's not worth dying for.'*

But Jared either didn't hear or was in another universe. He drove on, not wavering, refusing to budge, until Gary gave up and fell behind again. A few moments later Jared shot over the line, to the deafening cheers of the crowd and the roars of his team.

'I'll swear that man isn't afraid of anything,' Mr Vanner muttered. 'Did you ever see anything like that?'

Kaye couldn't answer. The violence of her own feelings terrified her. Jared's icy courage, his obstinate refusal to yield, might have cost him his life. Knowing that, he hadn't flinched. Now that it was over the truth hit her hard, and her heart was thundering.

She stayed quiet during the evening's celebrations. At dinner the television was on, showing a re-run of the race, with the commentator going berserk at the finish.

'Nerves of ice, nerves of steel. Can anything scare Jared Marriot?'

'For the love of heaven!' Jared exclaimed, embarrassed but grinning. 'It was nothing. I didn't even see him.'

This was greeted by disbelieving jeers, under cover of which Jared slipped away. Kaye went with him, and in the night that followed the distance between them shrank to nothing and she was almost content again.

Almost. The fear would be with her as long as she loved him. Which meant it would be with her always.

In the early hours she propped herself up on her elbow, regarding him tenderly as he slept. Now there was no need for words, except for those in her heart.

You gave it all back to me, she told him silently. Not just love, but trust and contentment, the confidence that I can feel safe in the world because it's a place where good things happen. I thought I'd lost it again recently, but you weren't well. That's all it was. If only I could tell you what you mean to me—a thousand times more than you meant before. Because now I can see into your heart and know that it belongs to me, and to our son. Last time I saw only emptiness there, but now—oh, my darling, now—Oh, heavens, why am I crying when I'm so happy?

She laid her face against his chest, listening to the soft beat of his heart, knowing that at last she'd come home to the place where she belonged—the only place in the world that mattered.

Softly she ran her fingertips over him, half fearing, half hoping to awaken him.

'I love you,' she said aloud. 'I've loved you for years, but I didn't dare admit it to myself. Now I can, and soon—oh, please, soon—I can admit it to you.'

He made a sound, and she looked up to find his face turned towards her, eyes still closed, lips very slightly parted. She smiled, laying a gentle kiss on them.

'But not yet,' she told him. 'You're not quite ready, are you? It's all there inside, but we're both waiting for the right moment. When will it come? That's a mystery, but we can be patient.' She smiled in self-mockery. 'I'm very good at waiting.'

She kissed him again, preparing to slide down in the bed and snuggle up to him. But suddenly he gave a long, sighing moan, then another. His head began to twist from side to side and the sound grew deeper, more intense and painful.

'Hush, darling,' she said, giving him a little shake. 'Wake up. I'm here.'

But his eyes didn't open, and she could tell that she hadn't reached him. The noise became softer, less anguished. Perhaps the bad moment was passing and it would be better to let him sleep. She watched him anxiously, trying to decide.

'No,' he groaned. 'No, no—I can't bear it—'

'Darling—' She tried to take him in her arms but he thrust her away, beginning to writhe.

'It isn't me—it can't be—it isn't me. No—no—*no!*'

His voice became a roar. His arms were flailing dementedly and she had to dodge them to get close to him.

'Wake up,' she cried. *'Wake up!'*

But it seemed as though he couldn't wake. Whatever the hellish place deep in inside him, he was trapped in it, screaming for release but unable to find it.

'Jared,' she cried, shaking him. 'I'm here—look at me. I'm going to make it all right.'

'It'll never be all right,' he growled, but still his eyes were closed and she couldn't tell if he knew she was there.

'Some things can't be put right. Nothing will ever be right again—never—never—'

'Yes, it will,' she urged. 'We can make it right as long as we're together. Wake up, darling, *please*.'

With a loud cry he sat up sharply in bed, eyes wide and staring, his entire body shaking violently. Appalled, Kaye kept hold of him, knowing that this was no ordinary nightmare. But when she tried to draw him close he thrust her away.

'Who the hell are *you*?' he shouted. 'Get out—get out! *Don't touch me!*'

'Jared, it's me—Kaye.' Hurriedly she switched on the light, which seemed to work.

As he returned to reality he seemed to collapse, then threw himself back on the bed.

'Do you know who I am?' she asked, sitting beside him.

He stared at her from dead eyes. 'Yes. It's all right. I'm awake now. I'm sorry if I hit you.'

'You didn't know what you were doing. It must have been a terrible dream. You were shouting such things.'

'What?' he asked tensely. 'What was I shouting?'

'You kept saying, "It isn't me." I don't understand.'

He gave a grunt. 'Oh, that again. It's because I was ill—face swelled up—and looking into the mirror was terrible.'

'You mean that crash you had at the start of the season? You injured your face?'

He seemed to hesitate. 'Not exactly. I crashed because I was ill, and I looked so dreadful I couldn't endure the sight of myself. It made me realise that one day I'll be old and ugly.'

'Old, but never ugly,' she assured him.

'Oh, yes, it's there—waiting at the end of the road.'

'Tell me all about it.'

'I don't want to dwell on it. It's not a pleasant memory.'

'But if you keep it hidden inside you, perhaps that's why you have nightmares. If you told me about it, perhaps it would go away.'

'Nothing will make it go away,' he said hoarsely.

But she wouldn't accept that. Taking him in her arms, she said fiercely, 'Tell me! We'll fight it together.'

'Are you strong enough to fight my demons?' he whispered.

'What demons?' she asked. 'You're recovered now. The demons were sent packing.'

'Yes—yes, of course.'

'And as long as we're together I'm strong enough for anything. Look.' She clasped his hand. 'Did you ever feel such strength?'

He surveyed the delicate hand that lay in his and gave a wry smile.

'No, I don't think I ever did,' he said. 'It's awesome.' He closed his fingers over hers. 'I guess you'll keep me safe.'

Nobody who knew Jared only superficially, which meant everyone else in the world, would have believed he'd ever say such a thing.

She could feel violent tremors going through him, almost as though he was weeping, and her arms tightened protectively about him.

She was moving her hands as she spoke, caressing him softly, teasingly, trying to distract him from his misery. She felt him grow still, as though he couldn't believe what was happening, then gradually the life seemed to be restored to his ravaged body. She enticed him more, luring him on to respond, until he did, moving his hands in an exploration that was almost tentative, then growing in confidence, until at last he cast diffidence aside and raised himself up to look down directly into her face.

He must have seen something there that he needed, for the next moment he was making love to her with full force. Kaye sighed with satisfaction. It had worked. She'd released him from his fears as only she could do. Her smile was one of triumph, melting into pleasure as he took possession of her with a vigour that was almost ferocity and which thrilled her.

'Go to sleep now,' she murmured. 'Everything's going to be all right.'

She believed it. Falling asleep in his arms, she thought that a new dawn had arrived for them.

CHAPTER FIVE

SHE awoke an hour later and lay with her eyes closed, relishing this new joy, then reaching across the bed for him.

But he wasn't lying there. Opening her eyes, she found him sitting on the edge of the bed, his back to her.

That wasn't part of the dream.

'Hello,' she said.

He turned quickly and smiled. 'Are you all right?' he asked.

'Shouldn't I be asking you that? You were in a bad way.'

He rolled over to lie beside her. 'I want you to tell me something.'

He wanted her to say she loved him, she thought.

'Yes? What?'

'When I was shouting in my sleep, did I say anything particular?'

'Only what I told you before,' she said, coming down to earth. 'You kept saying "It isn't me."'

'Nothing else?'

'Not that I remember.'

'Are you sure?' he asked, sounding tense.

'Quite sure. Why? What are you afraid you said?'

He gave an awkward laugh. 'Don't be silly.'

She tried to lighten the atmosphere with a tiny joke. 'You didn't mention other women, I promise.'

He rose to the occasion, meeting her mood. 'Well, that's a relief.'

She managed a small laugh. 'So your terrible secret is still a secret.'

His smile faded. She could have sworn a tremor went through him, and it flickered across her mind that perhaps he really did have another woman.

Suddenly the winds were howling again. Such a betrayal would destroy her. She'd opened her heart to him a second time, but there could be no other chances.

But he instantly replied, 'Don't say that. There's nobody but you. I love you. There—I've said it.' He flung the words out like an accusation.

She touched his face. 'You've been fighting it, haven't you?'

'I suppose I have,' he growled.

The fear passed. What could possibly go wrong now? It was time to risk everything on the throw of the dice.

'I saw you with your mother's ring,' she said. 'I even dared to hope you were going to give it to me. But then you got that headache.'

He raised one crooked eyebrow. 'Are you proposing to me?'

'I guess I am.'

She'd struck the right note, enticing him without pressure. Now his good humour and self-confidence were venturing back. 'The truth is you don't want me,' he observed. 'You just want the ring.'

'Well, it's quite a ring. As soon as I saw it I knew it had to be mine—plus—well, plus anything else that went with it.'

'So that's what I am? An extra tagged on like a supermarket special offer?'

'That's putting it very well. In time I'll probably exchange you for vouchers.'

'What do I get in return?' he wanted to know.

'All my love, now and for ever. Of course you've always

had that—you just didn't know it. Come to think of it, I didn't really know it myself for a long time.'

'I warn you, I'll try your patience.'

'Don't worry. You always have. I've learned to cope.'

Grinning, he kissed her. But then humour faded, and there were no more words for a while.

So now it seemed that they were engaged, she mused later. Possibly the strangest proposal ever.

As they prepared to leave Jared said, 'Can we keep this our secret for a while? There are a lot of things to be settled before the world knows.'

Mike, she thought. He must be told everything first.

'Of course,' she agreed.

Unusually, the next race—in Hungary—was only a week away, leaving little time for personal life. But after that there was a three-week gap, which would be their chance to think of themselves.

It would have been lovely to celebrate their engagement with another baby, and as they flew back to England from Germany she allowed herself to hope that a faint sign would turn out to be significant.

She remembered how quickly she'd become pregnant last time. One brief encounter and within two weeks she'd had the first hint. It might happen that way again, and this time she would have the pleasure of telling Jared and seeing his happiness.

But the hint turned out to be a false alarm, leaving her disappointed.

Still, I'm older now, she reassured herself. It won't happen so quickly. We'll get there. Be patient.

The trouble was that she didn't want to be patient. She wanted the joy of going through a pregnancy with Jared at her side. It would happen. She promised herself that.

* * *

On the flight to Hungary she sat next to Mr Vanner, taking notes, concentrating on work.

'I can't tell you how I'm looking forward to three weeks after this without any races,' he sighed.

Smiling, she nodded. She too was looking forward to those three weeks.

For the first two days everything went as they'd hoped. Jared achieved the fastest practice time, and the fastest qualifying time, beating Gary into second place on the grid.

'Just wait until we race tomorrow,' she heard Gary mutter. 'Then you'll see.'

'Oh, leave it,' she told him, pausing as she gathered her things.

The great hangar was emptying fast, and she hurried to leave.

'Well, bless my soul—look who it is.'

Looking up, Kaye saw a face she recognised.

'Hello, Tony. What brings you here?'

Tony Williams was a journalist whom she'd sometimes met, hanging around, trying to sniff out a good story, preferably a scandal. He was pleasant enough, but she was always on her guard.

'Just seeing if there was anything interesting going on,' he said airily.

'Well, there isn't.'

'Not so sure about that. There's a rumour going around about a certain person who had a mysterious spell in hospital a few months ago. It was a private hospital, nobody was allowed near, and no questions could be asked.'

Jared had already told her a little about this, but nothing would make her satisfy the journalist's curiosity, so she merely shrugged.

'It just makes you wonder,' Tony continued, 'why the nature of that illness is being kept so determinedly secret.'

'Possibly because it's nobody else's business,' she flashed.

'That's understandable. Especially if it was mumps.'

Jared hadn't given his illness a name, had merely spoken of his swollen face. With a monumental effort of will she froze her expression and kept quiet.

'You know what mumps does to a man, don't you?' Tony went on. 'It makes him sterile. Oh, he can still take a woman to bed, give her a good time, but nothing comes of it. She doesn't have to fear getting pregnant because he's useless.'

'Rubbish,' she managed to say.

'It's not. I knew a man once who had it happen to him. He'd been quite a Romeo in his day, so he went round looking up old girlfriends, hoping to find that he was already a father. It makes you wonder what he told those girls.' He struck an attitude. 'Hiya, honey, nice to see you again. Did you by any chance have my kid? No? Oh, well, on to the next one.''

She fought to keep her smile in place, knowing that he was watching her for any reaction.

'Sorry, Tony, but you're dreaming.'

'How would you know? You're not denying that he's Mike's father, are you? Everyone knows that Jared turned up suddenly, and you have to wonder why?'

'No, what *you* have to do is jump to a lot of glib conclusions. Jared's an honest man. He'd never do what you're suggesting. Vanish, if you know what's good for you.'

'Oh, come on, Kaye. It all fits. There's a great story here, and we'd pay a good price for it. All you have to do is— Hey, that hurt!'

'It was meant to. Get out, and if you print one word of this I'll make you sorry you were born.'

'So much for a free press—*ow*!'

'Now will you go?' she demanded.

'Frankly, Jared has my sympathy. I can see you're going to make him pay. All right, all right—I'm going.'

He vanished, leaving her alone, staring ahead, her mind filled with flashing, screaming images.

She would have given anything to be able to disbelieve this, but every instinct in her recognised it as the truth.

The time she'd seen Jared watching her in the car park; his sudden arrival at the pageant. Those weren't accidents. He'd come to find her—no, he'd come to find Mike. As Mike's mother, she was no more than a necessary extra, and Jared had done what he had to in order to secure them both.

That was all there was to it.

She forced herself to move. Outside, everyone was gathering, ready to go for a meal. Jared smiled when he saw her, the perfect picture of a man happy in love. You would believe it if you didn't know the truth.

'I won't join you for the meal,' she said. 'I want an early night.'

'Me too,' Jared said.

'No, I think Mr Vanner needs a chat with you,' she said quickly. 'I'll see you later.'

'Are you all right?' he asked, frowning as he glanced at her face.

'Yes, I'm fine. Bye.'

She fled—hoping that he wouldn't follow her, because she desperately needed to be alone to sort this out, but irrationally disappointed when he didn't insist. He would get deep into talk about the coming race and forget her existence until she was useful again.

She took a taxi, meaning to go to the hotel, but suddenly she couldn't bear to be enclosed by walls and she made the driver stop near a park. She would wander and try to cope with the way her world had collapsed. With all her heart she longed to deny it, but everything fitted too well. She'd been a fool. The man who always demanded his own way had made use of her.

The light was fading. She turned her steps towards the hotel, wondering what she was going to do when she saw Jared. Tell him? Ask him?

Not now, she thought. Don't distract him the night before a race. I'll go to bed and he'll find me 'asleep'. Tomorrow—when he's won—maybe—

But as she reached the corridor Jared's door opened, to reveal him, frowning.

'Where have you been?' he demanded.

'Just—for a walk.'

'A strange way to take an early night. I was worried about you. I dashed back to make sure you were all right, but you weren't here.'

'I needed to be alone for a while.'

He stood back to let her in, closing the door with a firmness that reminded her uncomfortably of a prison door slamming. This was a man she didn't know, with a tight face and hard, suspicious eyes.

'Alone?' he repeated.

'Yes. Alone.'

'What about Tony Williams?'

'*What?*'

'He's been seen around here, trying to rake up dirt about me. Are you saying you haven't spoken to him?'

Totally stunned, she stared at him as the world disintegrated for the second time that day.

'Answer me, Kaye. Have you been talking to that man or not? I want to know.'

'And I'll tell you,' she said, in a voice that was so quiet it was dangerous. 'But not if you speak to me like that. I will not be interrogated like a suspect—do you understand?'

Good resolutions were forgotten as her temper flared. It was a shock to find that Jared could provoke her like this, but something in his attitude had brought rage screaming to the surface.

'Do you understand?' she repeated.

'Yes, I think I understand. Evidently you have something to tell me.'

'Tony Williams came to see me at the track, spreading stories, dropping hints. I told him to leave. When he didn't I insisted. He was rubbing his face when he left.'

'You hit him?'

'Twice. I didn't mean to, but he was saying things about you that I couldn't bear. Now I'm going to bed.'

'What things?'

She took a long breath. 'Now isn't the time,' she said at last.

'Kaye, what did—?'

'Goodnight, Jared.'

'No!' He seized her arm as she tried to pass. 'We can't leave it like this.'

'We can, because I don't want to talk tonight.'

'Do you think you can just walk out on me like this? Do you think I'll allow it?'

'I'm not asking you to allow anything. I don't need your permission. Just for once you're not in charge, Jared.'

He flinched as though she'd struck him over the heart, and when she turned away he didn't try to stop her. She ran to her own room, slammed her fists against the wall and stayed there, motionless, for a time she couldn't count.

As last she pulled away and went to sit in a chair by the window. Outwardly she was calm, but inside she was sobbing.

There was a knock at her door. 'Please let me in.'

'Go away.'

'No. I'll stay here all night if I have to.'

Wearily she unlocked the door, immediately returning to the chair and sitting facing away from him.

He entered quietly, coming over and dropping to one knee beside her chair.

'Forgive me,' he murmured. 'I should never have spoken to you like that.'

He pressed his face against her. She could feel his warmth, but he still felt a million miles away. She didn't move.

After waiting for her to enclose his head in her hands he drew back, understanding the silent message.

'Tell me,' he murmured. 'I have to know everything.'

'All right.' She sighed. 'Tony Williams came to the pits

today. I think he was waiting to get me alone. He told me about the mumps and how it could have left you sterile. He said he knew someone who'd gone looking up old girlfriends, hoping to find that he was already a father.' She gave a bleak laugh. 'Who could imagine that?'

He flinched, rising to his feet, needing to get away from the blast of hostility that came from her, cursing himself for stupidity and blindness.

'You never told me the name of your illness, but it *was* mumps, wasn't it?'

'Yes.'

'And it left you sterile?'

'Yes.' His voice was almost inaudible.

'That day you turned up suddenly, it wasn't an accident, was it?'

'No.'

'How long had you known about Mike?'

'Only a short time. Hal showed me a picture of his family and you were in it. He told me about Mike and I realised—'

'That he was your son.'

'I thought he could be. Hal mentioned his birthday party, and the date told me he'd been born nine months after we were together.'

'You remembered the date that well? Oh, but of course—it was three days after the race in Japan, so naturally you'd remember. How convenient.'

He winced at her coldly ironic tone.

'I've never known you like this before. It isn't you.'

She rose and confronted him, meeting his eyes directly. 'How would you know, Jared? You have no idea who the real me is. All you know is the compliant me, ready to do or be anything you want because when you're there she can't think straight. But this is me too—a woman who doesn't like being taken for a fool.'

'I didn't—'

'Don't lie to me. Why did you suddenly turn up after years when you hadn't shown any curiosity?'

'I had no idea that I'd left you pregnant.'

'And of course you couldn't go back to find all the girls you'd snapped your fingers at—even if you could remember them all.'

'I told you I thought I'd stopped in time, and then I never heard from you—but it was my fault. I was careless.'

'And then you heard about Mike and you realised that everything might not be over. You even spied on me. That day in the school car park, I thought I imagined that I saw you—but you were there, watching me.'

'I wanted to be sure I'd got the right person,' he groaned.

'Why didn't you tell me the truth?' she asked desperately.

'Do you imagine I could have?'

'*Yes!* Perhaps not at first, but later. It's what you'd have done if we'd been as close as I thought we were. But I see now that we weren't. All this time you've been playing a clever game to pull me in, so that you can use me to claim your property. I have something you want, and you worked out how to get it. That's what you always do. Remember telling me that?'

'That may have been true once,' he said. 'And I won't deny that Mike is my best chance of being a father, and that's why I approached you at first. *But only at first.* Kaye, for pity's sake, don't you remember how things were between us from the moment we met again?'

'No!' she cried in pain. 'I only remember how you made me think they were. But it was all lies. Everything was lies. Even when—'

She stopped, choked by her tears.

'I swear it wasn't,' he said passionately. 'When I said I loved you I was telling the truth. When we met again, I never dreamed it would be like this between us. I thought it was all over, but then I knew it was you I wanted. Not just for Mike, but because you're the one. I love you. I've never said it before—not meaning it, anyway. With the others it was just a form of showbiz, but with you it's real.'

With all her soul she longed to believe him. But his betrayal of her trust was a torture that she couldn't get past.

'I don't believe you,' she said stubbornly. 'This is just part of the act.'

'Don't say that!' he cried. 'I know I should have told you the truth before. All this time I've been trying to find the right moment, and I nearly managed it, but then you said you wanted more children and I backed off because I was scared.'

'You? Scared? Don't make me laugh.'

'Scared. Terrified. You can't imagine. When you said that I saw myself as I must look to a woman now: useless, half-crippled, empty. *Not a real man*. Of course you want more children. You're a mother, with a mother's instinct, and you want a man who can help you fulfil that instinct. But I can't.' His voice rose in anguish. 'Don't you understand that?'

'It doesn't matter.'

'That's not what you said then.'

'*Nothing* would matter if you'd told me the truth, because we would have been so close that I wouldn't have cared about anything else. But you kept apart with your secret, and now I don't know who you are.'

As if from a great distance she saw a terrible look on his face: blank, despairing, helpless.

Why, she thought desperately, didn't his words affect her? Why didn't her love cause her heart to melt for him? But she felt as though a cage had slammed shut, trapping her inside. She was blind and deaf to his suffering, knowing only one thing: he had lied to her, tricked her. In her present bitter state, it seemed that never for one moment had he been honest with her. And that meant there was only a wilderness between them.

She began to walk back and forth, arms folded across her chest as though to protect herself from something, seeking a way out of the misery that engulfed her. But there was no way.

'So many things have suddenly become clear,' she said.
'When you had that nightmare you asked what you'd said in
your sleep. You kept insisting. I didn't understand, but you were
afraid you'd given away the secret, weren't you?'

Dumbly, he nodded.

'It was always there,' she continued. 'Behind every thought
or word or action. Always you were having to keep the important part of yourself to one side, never letting me suspect it. In
the end it became you. The real you. And I never guessed.'

She rubbed her hand over her eyes. 'I think you should go
now.'

'How can I leave things like this?'

'I don't think either of us has a choice. We can't settle anything tonight, and you have a heavy day tomorrow. You've got
to win that race.'

He stared at her. Did she really think he cared about that?

'Kaye—'

'Please go.' She opened the door and stood beside it until he
walked past into the corridor. But at the last moment he stopped
and tried to reach for her.

'Kaye, please—'

'Goodnight, Jared.'

He was facing a closed door.

Her dread, as she went to the track next morning, was that
Tony Williams might be there. She couldn't see him, but for
safety's sake she maintained a normal air—talking, smiling,
working as usual.

Jared did the same, speaking to her politely about some
meaningless subject before heading for the car. As he walked
his heart was beating with tension, for he knew that something
was badly wrong.

In the past one of his strengths had been his clarity of vision,
as though the mere act of racing gave his eyes a new sharpness—not physical, but springing from the inner conviction
that here he was king. The outside world vanished and the

only reality was the track ahead, leading him on to inevitable victory.

But now that clarity had gone, leaving only confusion. Where was he—and why? The engineer spoke on his radio.

'Time to move. Good luck.'

Suddenly he couldn't think of the words to say, so he raised his fist in a gesture of agreement. First the warm-up lap. Useful. It would give his mind a chance to clear. Functioning on automatic, he went round the track until he reached the start again, and then settled in pole position.

What was Kaye doing at this moment? Watching him, as she always did? Or standing back, rejecting him in her heart as well as her mind? He tried to thrust her away. This was his world and he must concentrate. But it was desolate without her, and the track ahead was still vague.

A yell. The moment had come. The five hanging lights went out, and they were off. From the corner of his eye he could see Gary, trying to edge ahead by the first bend. His rival was still in a sulphurous temper—something which once would have delighted him, for he liked nothing better than a challenge.

But now he was assailed by weariness and a crashing sense of failure. He took the first bend, managing to keep his lead. His mirror showed Gary falling in behind him, coming too close.

One lap, then two. All would be well if only he could pull himself together, but his head was pounding. There was Gary, coming up beside him, still too close.

'Watch out for him!' The message came shrieking over his radio. *'He doesn't care what he does.'*

It was true. Gary was trying to intimidate him. Jared moved, but he was too late. The cars collided and he felt himself swept up to a great height before turning over and over and landing with a crash that blotted out the world.

He was totally alone. All around him stretched a wilderness— bleak, empty of all human life.

Until this moment he hadn't known what true isolation was, only that he hated it. Always he'd surrounded himself by people who talked and laughed, assured him that life was a reckless game. Now he was lost in the silence, and he was terrified.

Nothing had worked out as he'd expected. His plan had been to approach Kaye, claim Mike, then share the child with her. That way he would have a stake in the future without having to give too much of himself. He would win her confidence, set up a financial trust, then get to work on Mike, ensuring that the child's loyalty would always be his.

He'd even toyed with the idea of marrying her as a way of securing his property, but he'd left that idea in limbo. Marriage would involve a degree of honesty and explanation that he'd rather do without. Better to wait and see how things worked out.

But their meeting had changed everything. Kaye was still partly the impish girl he remembered, yet now she was many other things, and a thousand times more enchanting. It might be her few extra years' maturity, or perhaps the sadness of her experience, bearing a child without the father's support, sacrificing her career. She must often have felt abandoned, but instead of making her bitter it had given her an edge—a sweet, ironic knowingness that had mystified and captivated him in equal measure.

It shamed him to recall how he'd toyed with the idea of a cold-blooded marriage. His reactions in life were as swift as in a race, and in almost no time he'd known he wanted her, body, heart and soul. Not just for Mike. For herself.

That was when he'd known he had real problems.

He'd known he must tell her everything, but with a cowardice he'd never suspected he'd put it off and put it off. Once he'd nearly made it, slipping his mother's ring into his pocket in readiness. But then she'd begun to talk about more children and he'd backed off, vowing to find a more suitable time.

He'd been fooling himself. There would never be a good time, and by delaying he'd left her to hear it from another

source—the worst thing that could have happened. Her chilly
contempt had shattered him.

Suddenly he'd found himself facing a situation he didn't
know how to deal with—one he couldn't talk his way out of or
shunt aside by winning a race. Now his feelings were real and
terrible, and he must confront them. If only he knew how.

There was only one person who might be able to show him
the way, but she was the person he'd hurt most of all, and
the freezing contempt with which she'd ordered him off had
stunned him.

But now she seemed to be there with him, and what he saw
in her eyes was not contempt, but heartbreak. For him she'd
ventured out from behind her defences, daring to trust again
and grow close because she loved him. He'd betrayed that trust
and smashed her to the ground.

With all his heart he longed to seek her forgiveness and
make things right, but that would never be possible. A man
who couldn't forgive himself had no right to ask forgiveness
of the one he'd injured, and that was the burden he must carry
from now on.

Now he almost hoped she wouldn't be there when he opened
his eyes.

But she was, sitting with her head buried in her hands as
though engulfed by despair.

CHAPTER SIX

For an hour she'd sat by the bed, wanting to be the first thing Jared saw. Anger and bitterness had drained from her, obliterated by horror at his accident, for which she blamed herself. If only he would awake she would make it right, promise him a new start. All would still be well.

At last the strain overcame her and she buried her head in her hands. When she looked up he was watching her.

'Jared,' she whispered eagerly.

His gaze seemed to be fixed on her, but there was nothing in his eyes. She leaned forward, making sure he could see her.

'Jared.'

'Where am I?'

'In a hospital near the racetrack. They brought you here, and it's looking good. At least you're back with us.'

'I've had crashes before. No need to make a fuss. What happened to the race? Is it over?'

'Yes, Gary won. He's been here, doing the self-reproach thing for driving you off the track.'

'He didn't. I just lost concentration. No big deal.'

'But it was my fault too. I know that. I'm so sorry.'

He looked blank. 'About what?'

'Last night. I should have calmed things down, and we could have talked later. If you knew how I blame myself for letting it turn into a row.'

'Did we have a row?' he asked, frowning.

'Don't you remember?'

'All I remember about last night is an almighty headache.' He closed his eyes. 'And I've still got it.'

'I'm here if you need me.'

He frowned. 'Better if you get the plane home tonight, or Mike will worry. I'll see you in England.'

His eyes closed. It was like the slamming of a door.

He didn't want her, she realised. As for last night—had he really forgotten, or was that simply another way of rejecting her? It was natural for his memory to be clouded, but she was full of dread.

Knowing Mike would be watching the race in England, she'd called him earlier, trying to sound reassuring. Now she called him again with a cheerful tale of Jared's recovery.

'Is he coming home?'

'Not tonight, but I'm coming.'

'So he's really, really all right?'

'Yes, I promise you. I'd stay here if he wasn't.'

And if he wanted me, she thought sadly.

Later that night, at home with the family, she watched the item on the news.

'Luckily it's not serious,' the commentator declared, 'and Jared Marriot is expected back tomorrow.'

'Can we go to the airport?' Mike asked eagerly.

'No, darling. He'll want to go straight home and rest.'

She was afraid he would argue, but perhaps some note of strain in her voice held him silent. He was a perceptive child.

For the next few days she had no direct contact with Jared. He called Mike, who would eagerly relate every conversation to her, and she had to be satisfied with that, plus what she heard from Mr Vanner at work. At last Jared texted her, asking her to come to his apartment that evening.

He greeted her with a kiss—not passionate like others they'd shared in the past, but a peck on the cheek.

'We need to talk,' he said quietly, sitting her down. 'I wasn't ready before. Thank you for being patient with me.'

'Mr Vanner says you're going to start driving again. Are you sure you're well enough?'

'Yes, I was only shaken up, and I'm over that.'

'Jared, please can we forget the things we said that night? I can't forgive myself for quarrelling with you and endangering you—'

'But you didn't,' he said pleasantly 'I crashed in the race because I got headachy and confused.'

He paused, and she had the sense that he was bracing himself for a great effort. She longed to tell him not to worry, that all would be well, but the words wouldn't come. A barrier lay between them—partly her making, partly his.

'We never really had a chance to discuss what you found out about me,' he said at last. 'It's true. I'm sterile.'

'But is that certain? Can they really be so sure after just one night?'

He grimaced. 'The doctor tried to soften the blow a little. He said there was a minute chance that I might be able to father a child—'

'How minute?'

'Two or three percent. Even if that's true—and frankly I don't believe it—I'd be a fool to rely on it. Better to face reality now. For practical purposes, I'm dead. I should have told you at the start but I lost my nerve. I'm sorry about that, and I'm sorry you found out the way you did. I know that no words can make it right, but for what it's worth I apologise.'

'There's no need. I reacted badly. I lost my temper and I shouldn't have—'

'Why not? What happened was my fault. I forced that scene on you, although you tried to avoid it.'

'But—'

'Please!' He held up a hand to silence her, still keeping his distance. 'I've had a lot of time to think,' he said quietly. 'That's something I haven't done much of in my life, but I see some things clearly now. You can't live as I have without hurting people. You were right in everything you said—'

'Jared, please—'

'No, let me finish before my courage runs out.' He gave a bitter laugh. 'I find I don't have as much of that as I thought. Another discovery. Boy, I'm really learning things about myself. None of them pleasant.'

Kaye closed her eyes. It hurt her unbearably to hear him condemn himself. She could have saved him from this if she'd been a little kinder. Now she wanted to reach out and comfort him, but he wouldn't let her. That hurt more than anything.

'I should have been honest with you from the start,' he continued. 'I wasn't, because I only thought of what I wanted. That's the ugly truth. I wanted my son, as though it was only my decision and you had no rights. I treated you like a pawn in my plans. How's that for arrogance? I never gave a thought to how much I could hurt you, but then I didn't think I *could* hurt you. Then, when we met, things changed. I wanted you again and—no, you don't want to hear that. You don't believe it, and perhaps if I was you I wouldn't believe it either.'

He gave a faint, self-mocking laugh.

'I'm not good at this empathy business—getting into other people's heads and seeing how things look to them. But you've shown me how I look to you, and it isn't nice. Don't worry. I'm not going to bother you with any of that stuff again.'

'Does that mean you're leaving us?' she asked in horror. 'Going away from Mike?'

'No, I still want to be his father, but I promise to leave you in peace. I'll support you both, of course. The financial arrangements will stay in place, and the money will increase every year. All I ask is that you let me have some contact with him. Apart from that, I'll keep my distance.'

'Mike won't like that at all,' she said, her voice shaking. 'He won't want you to keep your distance—especially when he knows who you are.'

'I hope we'll grow close, but I want you to know that I'll never take advantage of that. You're the boss. You make the big decisions. I'll fit in with whatever you say.'

'Putting me in the driving seat?' she said, trying desperately to lighten the mood. 'That's your place and yours alone, remember?'

'Yeah, well, maybe a guy who keeps taking the wrong road shouldn't be in the driving seat,' he said wryly. Suddenly he covered his eyes with his hand, and spoke in a strained voice that might have been on the edge of tears. 'Leave it, Kaye. There's nothing more to say. I'll make the arrangements and then get out of your way.'

With all her heart she longed to tell him that she loved him, beg him to give their love another chance. But was it love? Could she be sure? Was this perhaps his way of claiming his share of Mike without commitment? Would he welcome her love or regard it as a nuisance?

The struggle that lay ahead of her now demanded clever strategy. She must be as subtle as that great driver Jared Marriot on a winning streak. And then perhaps she too would crossing the finishing line first.

'All right,' she said calmly. 'We'll do it however you wish. But we have some decisions to take together. How and when are we going to tell Mike, and when can he come and see you race?'

There were seven races left, but only the next two were in Europe. The ones after that were at a huge distance, and taking Mike wouldn't be practical.

'As your son he's entitled to the privilege,' Kaye persisted. 'It'll mean the world to him. The Belgian Grand Prix is the best choice. It's the last race before school starts.'

'All right,' he said uncertainly, as though her brisk tone had taken him by surprise. 'You seem on top of everything. I'll leave you to make the arrangements.'

She gathered her things, the very picture of an efficient administrator.

'Then I'll be going. I'm glad we got matters settled. It'll be so much better for Mike, and that's all that matters, isn't it? Goodbye.'

As he heard her go downstairs Jared turned the light off and stood by the window, watching her go through the smallest crack in the curtain. She might turn, and she must not be allowed to see him standing there lest she guess that his eyes followed her as obsessively as his thoughts.

He'd fought to seem cool tonight, but it had been hard. Something deep inside him still cried out to her, but he resisted it. A protective shield, developed over years of facing and surviving danger, had kept him safe. And he would make sure that it always did.

For his own sake, but mostly for her. He must set her free and never hurt her again.

She had reached the end of the street. Now she was turning, raising her head to look up at his window, but he'd stepped well back in the darkness, where she couldn't see him.

It was better that way.

Mike was over the moon at the news that he was to go to the Belgian Grand Prix. The arrangement was that the three of them should fly out the day before.

'Thank you for being so understanding,' Kaye said to Mr Vanner.

He grinned. 'We're all hoping. Whatever keeps Jared happy is good for the team.'

So it was an open secret. Smiles and warm looks came from the others, and she could see that what her boss said was true. They were all hoping that things would come right between her and Jared. There was even a hint that some of them were taking bets on it.

And it would never happen.

Sam and Ethel too were over the moon.

'I think Mike already knows,' Ethel whispered.

'You told him?'

'I didn't have to. The bond is there, and he's begun to feel it. Look at the way Jared keeps in touch, calling him almost every day. The truth won't come as a surprise. It's what Mike's hoping for.'

Kaye made the Belgian bookings, assigning separate hotel rooms to herself and Jared. When the day came everyone wished her luck as she set off.

On the plane Mike sat by the window with Jared next to him, deep in conversation. Occasionally one of them would appeal to her, but she tried not to intrude. This was their time.

If things had been different the next few days would have been a dream of family delight. For practice and qualifying Mike was watching in the stands, and when Jared won the race Mike and Kaye were so close to the podium that they were sprayed with champagne.

Later, in Jared's room, they feasted—just the three of them. Suddenly Mike looked at Jared, then at Kaye, then back to Jared.

'Are you my dad?' he asked.

Kaye held her breath. How would he deal with this approach?

Jared met his son's eyes. 'If you want me to be,' he answered quietly.

She relaxed. He'd done it perfectly.

With bouncing, shrieks and hugs, Mike indicated that this was just what he wanted. Kaye realised that Ethel was right. He'd suspected and longed for it to be confirmed. Now he was in seventh heaven. His family was complete. He had the father he wanted. Everything in his little world was wonderful.

'Are you going to get married?' he asked eagerly.

'No, darling,' Kaye said. 'We're just going to go on being friends. The only change will be that you'll have a father, and you'll see lots of him.'

'But—' He frowned, trying to take this in. 'You two—you go together—*yes you do*.'

'Yes, we do,' Jared agreed. 'We're very fond of each other and, like your Mum says, we're good friends. We don't have to be married. We have you, and that's all we need.'

'But I want you.'

'And I want you. You're my son, and we'll always have each other, whether we live in the same house or not.'

'But—'

'Not now. Let's talk about it another time. Tonight we just celebrate. Look, I've got something for you.' He produced a box from a drawer. 'You had a birthday recently. I missed that, so this is a belated present, and I'll never miss any more.'

'It's a cell phone,' Mike breathed.

'Your mother says your reading and writing are coming along really well, so we can text as well as call. Let me show you.'

Mike was an apt pupil, who needed to be shown things only once.

It was the best gift Jared could have given him, Kaye thought. But there was more to come. With a flourish Jared produced another gift—the most recent version of a game called Champion. It was played with dice and counters, and Mike eagerly undertook the task of instructing the other two.

Kaye joined in, saying and doing everything that would make the little boy happy, but part of her was standing aside, aching at the thought of how it might have been. Jared grew easier with Mike all the time, because somewhere deep inside him was a natural father eagerly making his way out, and it was a delight to see it emerge into the sunlight.

What a family they might have made if they could have been together always. But Jared would not agree, because he couldn't forgive her for their quarrel. In her initial rage she'd rejected him, and he'd turned that rejection back against her, unforgiving.

Now, for Mike's sake, she must smile and pretend that all was well. She would do whatever she had to, but inside she was divided between pleasure at her child's happiness and anger at Jared because it could have been so much better.

At last Mike began to nod off. Together they put him to bed and murmured goodnight to his sleeping form.

'He fought sleep to the last minute,' Jared said as they slipped out and closed the door. He was grinning.

'That's what they all do,' Kaye said. 'You'll soon find out.'

'I'm looking forward to it.'

'So am I.'

She took a deep breath. With so much at stake it was worth one final effort.

'Jared, listen to me. This is urgent. I've been wondering if Mike has maybe seen things more clearly than we have. He's right that we belong together. I don't mean marriage, but I think it would be good for him if—if we lived under the same roof. It doesn't have to be a close relationship, if you don't want it, but let us be your home base—the place you come back to between trips abroad—so that Mike always knows he'll see you soon.'

But he was already shaking his head.

'It couldn't work. I've done you too much harm.'

'I told you that didn't matter,' she protested.

'I think it does, and you *know* it does. Whatever feeling there was between us, I've ruined it. Kaye, don't try to be kind to me. I betrayed your trust. I let you think everything was on the level while all the time—well, you understand. I damaged you, and I always will if I stay around you. I've come to see that it's the way I'm made. I can't change it, but I can back off to protect you.'

'Is that it?' she cried. 'Or do you blame me for the way I found out and the things I said? Do you hate for knowing the truth you tried to hide—?'

'No,' he said, almost violently. 'The only person I blame for anything is myself. Kaye, I'm doing this for *you*. I beg you to try to understand that. You're young—you'll meet another man who'll treat you properly and give you more children.'

'That doesn't matter—'

'You think it doesn't now, but later it will. I've seen you and Mike together. You're a fantastic mother, and that's an instinct you'll need to satisfy more than once. With me you never could.

Don't you understand that? I'm no good for you and I never will be. In time you'll come to hate me.'

'Don't tell me how I think and feel,' she said angrily. 'That's for me to say.'

'All right, I'll tell you something else. The day you found out that I hadn't been honest with you everything changed for you—as though a dark cloud had come over the world. Didn't it?'

'Jared—'

'Didn't it?' He was holding her shoulders and now he shook them slightly. *'Didn't it?'*

'Yes—all right, yes. These last few years I've found it so hard to rely on people, and when you returned I kept my distance because I was being careful. But you overcame that and I found I could love you. I didn't want to, but it was as though the years had rolled back. Things I thought I could never feel again—closeness, confidence, belief in life and people—'

She stopped, hurt to the heart by the despairing resignation on his face.

'You felt those things again,' he said sadly, 'and then I destroyed them—*again*. And I always would. I won't let that happen. I've hurt you enough. I won't hurt you any more. From now on I'll live on the fringes of your life—just close enough to be a father to Mike, but not close enough to harm you.'

'You don't know what you're talking about,' she said desperately. She was losing him again. She didn't want him on the fringes of her life. She wanted him at the centre, in her heart.

'I know what I have to do—for both our sakes, for Mike's sake. You won't lose, Kaye. I'll see to that.'

She would lose everything, she thought, and he would never understand.

'You know nothing about what I'll lose,' she said bitterly. 'Let's have the truth, Jared. You're not doing this for me, but yourself. You don't love me, and you don't want to be encumbered by me.'

'Don't be stupid,' he raged. 'Of course I love you. I love you more than I can bear. Why can't you—?'

The door opened and Mike stood there, looking worried.

'Are you mad at each other?' he asked.

'Of course not,' Jared said with forced brightness.

Kaye was filled with inspiration.

'Well, actually, I am a bit annoyed at your father,' she said, managing a smile. 'We've been playing Champion again, and I think he's cheating. Fancy that!'

'But he doesn't need to cheat,' Mike said indignantly. 'He always wins everything he does.'

'Only because he cheats,' Kaye said, with a fair assumption of teasing indignation.

'I do not,' Jared returned, understanding what she was doing and falling in with it.

'You certainly do,' she insisted.

'Don't.'

'Do.'

'Don't.'

'Do.'

Relieved, Mike gurgled with delight as they squared up to each other, glaring with just the right amount of comic aggression.

'You've done me an injustice,' Jared declared.

'I don't think so.'

'I know so.'

'Oh, yeah?' he demanded.

'Yeah!'

'Yeah?'

'Yeah!'

They met each other's eyes, each sending a silent message of pain and farewell, so different from the laughing performance they were giving the child.

'I think I'd better give in,' Jared said. 'Your mother's a very determined lady.' He winked at his son. 'I'll bet you could teach me a thing or two about that game,' he said, 'but now it's time you were back in bed.' He gave Mike a hug. 'See you tomorrow. Goodnight, you two.'

He was gone before Kaye could say anything. She heard his footsteps going down the corridor, and his door closing.

Looking back, she could see how that evening had set the pattern. After their return to England any contact they had was all for Mike. On the night before he went back to school Jared called him, and next morning there was a text wishing him good luck.

A week later there was the Italian Grand Prix.

'Please, Mum,' Mike begged.

'No, darling. It's too soon after the start of term. I want you to concentrate on school.'

Even so, she thought she might have yielded if Jared had asked them to be there. But he hadn't.

'I blew it,' she told Ethel. 'You were right about me. I am judgemental. Otherwise we could have sorted it out quietly, he might not have had that crash, and then things would have been all right. But a curtain has come down in his mind and I can't get past it. Perhaps because he doesn't really want me to.'

'Or maybe fate still has a nice surprise for you?' Ethel suggested.

'I don't think that's going to happen. Life doesn't work that way.'

But she was wrong.

She discovered just how wrong she was on the night before the race. At first she couldn't take it in. The implications of what had happened were so tremendous that she could only sit and stare at the wall until Ethel came in, wanting to know what was up.

Kaye told her.

'Get going,' Ethel said at once. 'Call a taxi, go to the airport, catch the first plane you can.'

Dazed, she obeyed. In the early hours she was on her way to Italy, looking out of the aeroplane window at the darkness. So many nights she'd stared into that darkness in tearful despair, as much for Jared as for herself. Now she knew hope again—but with it the fear that hope might once more betray her.

'Please,' she whispered. 'Please—one more chance—for his sake—*please*.'

Nobody knew she was coming, and at the airport she queued for a taxi and gave the address of the track.

She arrived at the same time as several members of the team, who recognised her and steered her through Security.

'We thought you weren't coming to this one,' someone said.

'Something's happened. Where's Jared?'

She found him in the garage, inspecting the car with his race engineer and a few mechanics. He looked up, amazed at her entrance and at the determined look on her face.

'Is something wrong with Mike?' he asked.

'No, he's fine. This isn't about Mike. It's about us. In fact, it's about this.' She held up a small plastic strip. 'Do you know what this is? It's a pregnancy test, and it's positive. *I'm pregnant.*'

'You—you can't be.'

'Don't tell me what I can or can't be. I know that I am. I've suspected it for a few days and last night I did this test. It's positive.'

'Kaye—'

'Two or three percent, eh? Well, sometimes the numbers come up, and this time they have.' Keenly aware of the fascinated crowd gathering around them, she raised her voice. 'That's twice you've made me pregnant, and this time you're not going to escape.'

She was watching his face, seeing every fleeting feeling from disbelief to incredulous joy.

'Kaye—' he whispered. 'Kaye—don't say it unless you're sure—I beg you—'

She moved closer, murmuring so that only he could hear.

'That doctor told you there was still a tiny chance. Well, the chance was on our side.'

Suddenly inspiration came to her. Now she knew what she must do. Jared had suffered in his masculine pride, and now it was in her power to give it all back to him. If she did nothing else she would do this for him.

She raised her voice again, so that the crowd could hear and understand that this was a man who still had everything—could father a child, could hold his head up among other men.

'I'm pregnant, Jared. It didn't take you long, did it? Just a few weeks and here we go again. Well, this time you have to make an honest woman of me. Or I'm going to make an honest man of you. Whichever is the easier.'

Cheers and applause from the mechanics. She dropped her voice again.

'I won't take no for an answer. I know you don't love me, but—'

'Don't be so damned ridiculous,' he roared. 'Of course I love you. I'm mad about you. How could you be blind enough not to know that?'

'Well, I didn't,' she yelled back. 'You've kept it a mighty secret.'

'Nonsense. I've given myself away at every turn. Everyone else knows I'm crazy about you. Why don't you?'

'Maybe because you didn't want me to know?' she accused.

'You are one infuriating woman!'

'I need to be to put up with you. I never know where I am.'

'Then let's settle it,' he growled, and yanked her into his arms.

More cheers and applause, but neither of them heard, so totally absorbed were they in enjoying each other as they had thought never to do again. It was like being kissed for the first time, and yet being kissed by a man whose kisses she knew with every fibre of her being, and wanted to know for their rest of her life.

When they became aware of the joyful audience Jared pulled her aside into a tiny room.

'Are you sure?' he said urgently.

'Quite sure. You read that strip.'

'I don't mean that. Are you sure I won't harm you if—?'

'If you marry me? You're *going* to marry me. Haven't you understood that yet? You're mine. I claim possession. No argument. Now I'm in the driving seat—my foot on the accelerator, my hands on the wheel.'

'We go wherever you say,' he agreed.

'Think you can live with that?'

'I think it sounds wonderful,' he said fervently, discovering to his own surprise that he meant it.

He could have trusted no other woman in the world like this. But she knew everything about him: the best—his strengths, his determination, the power of his heart—and the worst—his weaknesses, the things he feared, the things he couldn't say and relied on her to know without words.

That knowledge gave her power over him, and he was content to have it so.

'Love, honour and obey,' he said, smiling faintly.

'Think you can manage all three?' she challenged.

'I guess I'll have to.'

'Let's call Mike.'

'Yes, let's. Then we'll talk to Sam and Ethel—ask them to start looking for a house big enough for all five of us.'

She gave him a joyful kiss, and made the call. From outside came cries of 'Why are we waiting?' and they went out to be smothered with cheers and embraces.

It was time for the race. Jared took off around the track, driving the race of his life, and when he sped triumphantly across the finishing line he knew that his family were with him, as now they would always be.

For the first time in years he was not alone, and he would never be alone again. It was his greatest victory.

* * * * *

Coming Next Month

Available July 12, 2011

#4249 HER OUTBACK COMMANDER
Margaret Way

#4250 NOT-SO-PERFECT PRINCESS
Melissa McClone
Once Upon a Kiss...

#4251 A FAMILY FOR THE RUGGED RANCHER
Donna Alward
Rugged Ranchers

#4252 GIRL IN A VINTAGE DRESS
Nicola Marsh
The Fun Factor

#4253 FROM DAREDEVIL TO DEVOTED DADDY
Barbara McMahon

#4254 SOLDIER ON HER DOORSTEP
Soraya Lane
Heroes Come Home

You can find more information on upcoming
Harlequin® titles, free excerpts and more at
www.HarlequinInsideRomance.com.

HRCNM0611

USA TODAY *bestselling author B.J. Daniels*
takes you on a trip to Whitehorse, Montana,
and the Chisholm Cattle Company.

RUSTLED

Available July 2011 from Harlequin Intrigue.

As the dust settled, Dawson got his first good look at the rustler. A pair of big Montana sky-blue eyes glared up at him from a face framed by blond curls.

A woman rustler?

"You have to let me go," she hollered as the roar of the stampeding cattle died off in the distance.

"So you can finish stealing my cattle? I don't think so." Dawson jerked the woman to her feet.

She reached for the gun strapped to her hip hidden under her long barn jacket.

He grabbed the weapon before she could, his eyes narrowing as he assessed her. "How many others are there?" he demanded, grabbing a fistful of her jacket. "I think you'd better start talking before I tear into you."

She tried to fight him off, but he was on to her tricks and pinned her to the ground. He was suddenly aware of the soft curves beneath the jean jacket she wore under her coat.

"You have to listen to me." She ground out the words from between her gritted teeth. "You have to let me go. If you don't they will come back for me and they will kill you. There are too many of them for you to fight off alone. You won't stand a chance and I don't want your blood on my hands."

"I'm touched by your concern for me. Especially after you just tried to pull a gun on me."

"I wasn't going to shoot you."

Dawson hauled her to her feet and walked her the rest of the way to his horse. Reaching into his saddlebag, he pulled out a length of rope.

"You can't tie me up."

He pulled her hands behind her back and began to tie her wrists together.

"If you let me go, I can keep them from coming back," she said. "You have my word." She let out an unladylike curse. "I'm just trying to save your sorry neck."

"And I'm just going after my cattle."

"Don't you mean your boss's cattle?"

"Those cattle are mine."

"*You're* a Chisholm?"

"Dawson Chisholm. And you are…?"

"Everyone calls me Jinx."

He chuckled. "I can see why."

Bronco busting, falling in love…it's all in a day's work.
Look for the rest of their story in

RUSTLED

Available July 2011 from Harlequin Intrigue
wherever books are sold.

Harlequin *Presents*

THE NOTORIOUS
WOLFES

A powerful dynasty,
where secrets and scandal never sleep!

Eight siblings, blessed with wealth, but denied the one
thing they wanted—a father's love. Haunted by their
past and driven to succeed, the Wolfes scattered to the
far corners of the globe. It's said that even the blackest
of souls can be healed by the purest of love....

But can the dynasty rise again?

Beginning July 2011

A NIGHT OF SCANDAL—*Sarah Morgan*
THE DISGRACED PLAYBOY—*Caitlin Crews*
THE STOLEN BRIDE—*Abby Green*
THE FEARLESS MAVERICK—*Robyn Grady*
THE MAN WITH THE MONEY—*Lynn Raye Harris*
THE TROPHY WIFE—*Janette Kenny*
THE GIRL THAT LOVE FORGOT—*Jennie Lucas*
THE LONE WOLFE—*Kate Hewitt*

8 volumes to collect and treasure!
